Little
ROSE

Josephine Blake

xoxo,

The Brittler Sisters Series

Book 2

To sign up for Josephine Blake's mailing list, please visit her
website. You will be kept up to date on all sales and new
releases.

http://www.awordfromjosephineblake.com

For *all* My Little Adventurers
With all My Love

Chapter One

For My Loved Ones,

I miss you. It's been a long time since I left Manhattan, and I am anxious for news. Tell me what has happened in your lives. Spare no details in your response and I will spare none as I tell you what has been happening in mine.

Dianna paused to run the tip of her fountain pen over her bottom lip as she thought. She sat at the scrub kitchen table, her ankles crossed beneath her faded brown skirts.

She'd been out of touch with her family for the past year and could only imagine their anxiety for her. It wasn't as though Dianna had had any choice. It wasn't easy to mail regular correspondence when you were on the run from murderous natives.

Dianna exhaled violently, her blonde curls blowing away from her face as she did so. She looked around the tiny cabin, breathing in the earthen scent from the pine logs that had built it. It was comprised of one room. The kitchen sat to the left of her. The bed, a few paces away on her right. Between the dining area, where Dianna now sat, and the bed was a small stone fireplace. Within it sat a char-black pot, hung from an iron peg.

It was a small space, but it was home, and it had been for almost an entire year. The quilt on the bed was handmade and bore an embroidered pattern of leaves across its brown and gray surface.

Dianna heaved another sigh and then smiled as her eyes fell onto the cradle that sat at the foot of the bed. It was made of sturdy wood of a deep red-brown color. Shiye, Dianna's husband, had carved intricate pictures on both the head and footboard. Two crossed feathers, surrounded by a twisting garland of oak leaves, decorated the head. A single feather surrounded by a garland of pine branches sat upon the foot.

"You see?" Shiye had told her, tracing his finger over one of the feathers. "One is for you, one is for me. The other is for our child."

Her husband's words seemed to echo in her mind for a moment, and Dianna sent up a silent prayer for his safe return. Shiye had gone on one of his frequent trips, hunting and scouting the area for signs of danger. He was likely on his way home now; he'd been gone for several days.

Dianna laid an exhausted hand on her stomach to feel the reassuringly warm fumblings of her baby.

"You'll be as warm-blooded as your papa, sweetheart," she whispered to her belly. She stood with a groan and strode over to the window to pull open the shutters. Sweat was beading on her forehead, though the spring night was relatively mild. Stars twinkled on the surface of the nearby river, making it appear as though thousands of fireflies lay trapped beneath the rippling water.

She was on the point of turning back to her letter when a movement out of the corner of her eye caught her attention and she stopped. She stared hard at the shadows of the surrounding trees. Nothing shifted in the blackness, but Dianna's spine itched with discomfort.

"Shiye?" she called hesitantly into the night. Her right hand wandered over the back of her waistband and she pulled a small throwing knife from its sheath there. "Who's there?" she called again. A delicate fawn slipped out of the undergrowth a few feet away and Dianna let out a sigh of relief. Replacing the knife Shiye had given her in its leather scabbard, she turned away from the window and sat back down at the table to continue her letter.

Greyson Crowley and I were not meant to be. I must confess that I was too blinded by the excitement of my journey to note that the man was an obvious drunkard, a liar, and a scoundrel. Fortunately for me, we were unable to marry upon my arrival in Cheyenne, and I was still unattached to him upon my discovery of his true nature.

I spent some time recovering from a head injury inflicted upon me by the wretched man, and it was during this time that I met my new husband. His name is Shiye, and it was he who found me after Greyson Crowley's drunken antics nearly ended my life. Shiye saved me and aided me in my recovery. Soon after, we were married in Cheyenne.

I cannot tell you where I am now, for fear of this letter falling into the wrong hands. Shiye has been falsely accused of a terrible crime by his people and we are, to the best of my knowledge, still being pursued by them.

I will tell you that I am happy. For not only have I discovered a wonderful and loving husband, I am also with child. I hope someday soon, we can arrange to meet somewhere so that I might get to see you all. I miss you more than words can say.

I am so sorry that I lost touch with you over the

course of my ventures. I hope you will forgive me. I desire nothing more than to see your smiling faces, and I think of you always.

> *Yours forever,*
> *Dianna*

There. That sounded alright. Though there was no guarantee that her family would respond to her letter, Dianna was desperate to make contact with them. She felt horrible about leaving them without any information or means of contacting her and could only hope that they would forgive her and write back with haste.

There came a steady crunch of footsteps outside the cabin and Dianna tensed again, reaching for her knife. The footsteps stopped and Dianna heard a grunt, followed by the thud of something large being tossed to the ground. She smiled, her body relaxed, and she stood to open the front door.

Shiye was bent double, his hands busy in a small bag of supplies at his feet. Next to him, bloody and gutted, lay a string of rabbits, a few featherless birds, his hunting knife and his bow. At the sound of the door opening, he straightened and opened his arms just in time, for Dianna had flown at him with enough force to nearly knock him flat. Without giving him a moment to catch his breath, she kissed him.

Shiye chuckled beneath her lips and his arms encircled her. "I have missed you as well," he said pleasantly. Dianna clung to him fiercely. Feeling such a powerful wave of happiness that, for a moment, she couldn't speak. Shiye's welcome heat radiated into her skin, warming parts of her soul that always grew cold in his absence. Before her pregnancy, Dianna had always gone on these short expeditions with him. Now though, the idea was quite out of the question.

"I expected you back days ago," she said angrily, pulling away from her husband to confront him with a furious stare. "What happened?" He was only thirty and two to Dianna's twenty-nine years, but his dark eyes were ringed with an age that only terrible trial can bring. Over the last year or so, this look had lessened slightly. He had grown content and—Dianna hoped—he had begun to forgive himself for the terrifying events in his past that had been out of his control.

Shiye's high brow fell in a look of irritation. "I found signs of passing and tracked them over the mountains. It was likely only a traveler, but I needed to be certain. They were close to us, but they seem to have left the area."

Dianna felt a distinct sense of unease grow in her belly. The baby squirmed. She lay a protective hand over the wiggling in her stomach and bit her lip. "Are you sure? We haven't had anyone come this way for a long time, should we...?"

"We're safe," Shiye cut her off. His hands came to rest over hers, and he smiled down at her. "I tracked them a long time. Whoever it was headed East, away from Cheyenne. If it were a tracker, they would have headed back to the village to bring the others, not East."

Dianna felt her shoulders relax, and she smiled up at Shiye as the baby gave another firm kick to their joined hands. Shiye crouched down in the dirt to press a kiss to Dianna's belly. "I missed you both," he whispered, wrapping his hands around Dianna's lower back and pressing his ear to her stomach. Dianna giggled as she felt the baby jolt once more, pressing against Shiye's cheek.

"Welcome home," she whispered. Shiye stood and swept his long hair over his shirtless back. Dianna took the time to run her fingertips over the well-shaped muscles of his chest and stomach as he pulled her into his body once more. His skin was dark and smooth, like melted caramel. His eyes were a rich hazel, and at the moment they were burning with a steady heat. Dianna felt as though she had stepped through the doors of a warm candy shop. His scent filled her nostrils so that he was all there was in the world, and when he kissed her again, it was a long time before either of them moved at all.

"I need a bath," he chuckled at last, gesturing to his general state of unkemptness. Dianna looked down at his filthy clothes with the air of a professional seamstress. Shiye's britches were made of a soft animal hide. He regularly switched back and forth between them and woolen trousers, often accompanied by a long-sleeve cotton shirt. However, when he hunted, he always wore leathers.

"It's late, dear, come to bed. We'll deal with everything else in the morning."

Shiye shrugged. "I'll only be a short time. You go back in the house. I'll finish up here and you can warm some dinner?" he asked hopefully, as his stomach gave a thunderous growl. Dianna laughed and leaned forward on her tiptoes to press her lips to his once more. Her eyes slid hungrily over his strong, unshaven jaw and high cheekbones, and he looked back at her with an equal hunger. His almond-shaped eyes narrowed and he gave her a playful swat on the bottom as she walked away from him. Dianna made sure to sway her hips as much as she could in her current state and looked back just before she entered the cabin to give her husband a small wink.

As she stoked the fire and heated Shiye's dinner, she listened to the sounds of her husband puttering outside the walls of their home. She hummed a little as she did so, thinking that tonight would be the first night in over a week that she might actually get some decent sleep. After a time, she heard the sounds of splashing and went to peer through the open window.

Shiye had sunk to his neck in the slow-moving river and was swimming vigorously. His clothes lay abandoned on a patch of boulders next to the water. It was a mild night, but the river was always cold. Dianna went outside to bring a few more logs in for the fire, knowing how Shiye would shiver when he finally joined her indoors. She watched him out the window for a few more moments, her arms folded comfortably over her chest, then she approached the riverbank and sat down on an outcropping of rocks, allowing her bare feet to drift in the small pools that formed there. Shiye was scrubbing himself with a rough piece of cloth, his shoulders shaking with cold.

"Won't you join me?" he asked, holding out a trembling hand in sarcastic invitation. Dianna looked up at the snow-capped mountain in the distance and shook her head.

"I'd rather keep my fingers and toes, thank you very much," she chuckled. The river was fed by melting snow and mountain streams. The water never reached a pleasant temperature until late summer.

Shiye shrugged dismissively, as though he could stand to lose a few extra fingers and toes, and he climbed from the water. It puddled around his feet as he reached for the dry towel Dianna had carried out with her. Then, hair still sopping, arms covered in goosebumps, Shiye gathered his clothes and led Dianna by the hand into the warm cabin, shutting the door behind them.

An hour later, Shiye sat on the hearth, finishing his dinner while Dianna darned a pair of trousers from his bag. She tied the ends off and set her sewing kit aside, looking down sadly at the few remaining spools of thread within.

"Do you think you could travel to town soon?" she asked quietly, "We're running low on several things... We could trade the furs for what we need, and I-" she hesitated, watching her husband carefully for his reaction. "I've written a letter I'd like to post as soon as possible."

Shiye looked up at her. The firelight danced over his broad shoulders. His hips were sloppily encased in the towel he had used earlier. "A letter," he said. His voice was thoughtful, not doubtful, or even reprimanding. He seemed to be considering the idea.

"I thought we might give the post office as a return address," she whispered hopefully, running her fingers over the softness of the quilt upon which she sat.

Shiye combed his fingers through his long, damp hair for a moment, his eyes on the flickering flames. "It's been a long while since we have seen any signs of pursuit," he said after a moment, "We're a long way from the place where I grew up." He shifted his eyes onto Dianna, who was twirling a loose thread between her thumb and forefinger, not looking at him.

"I don't see any reason we could not write your family and let them know you are safe."

Dianna stood excitedly and hopped over to the table. Her letter lay there, folded in thirds, and she picked it up to show her husband. Shiye glanced at it, and after a moment, he nodded.

"We should let them know you are safe," he muttered with half of a shrug. Dianna moved forward and wrapped her arms around him.

"I love you," she said, snuggling her nose into the nape of his neck. Shiye sighed and his palm came up to cradle the back of her head.

"I love you, as well."

Their tiny cabin was located about a three days' ride from the closest town. They were now in possession of two horses. Tawny, who was technically gifted to Dianna by Greyson Crowley when she was to be his wife, and Tanulonli, whom Shiye had purchased shortly after leaving Cheyenne. They also owned a cantankerous old mule that went by the name of Samson.

Shiye and Dianna had taken many long trips to town since they'd decided to settle here. The small community of Buffalo Creek had been far more accepting of their unusual relationship than Cheyenne had been. Though the townspeople didn't necessarily welcome them with open arms, most were at least, kind enough to give a small smile in passing. At the most, the uncomfortable people in the village avoided eye contact, and skirted around Shiye as he made his way through the streets.

As Dianna was now several months pregnant, the idea of her accompanying her husband was quite out of the question. Her pregnancy hadn't been what you would call comfortable, but she had been having an easier time than she had first expected. Her morning sickness had long since abated, and she was stronger than she had been in the early days of her pregnancy. Now, eight months on, she was encumbered and weary, but capable. Dianna was acutely aware that there was much more of her than usual, and she was itching to hold her new child in her arms. It wasn't only her excitement at the idea of becoming a new mother, she was beyond ready for the baby to come. Her body was heavy, her brain was mush, and her ankles and feet were continuously swollen. She frequently walked the short distance to the river to cool them in the icy water.

Other than the basic cooking and cleaning, she was relieved of any other duties. Shiye would hardly allow her to lift a finger. He'd been this way since he'd first discovered his wife was pregnant, and his position had not shifted in the slightest as time elapsed.

Though Dianna was eager for her letter to start wending its way toward her family in Manhattan, she was not at all ready for Shiye to be on his way so soon after he had arrived home. It frustrated her that she was stuck in one place while he was off tending to important matters. Dianna had been a fixture beside her husband since they had first met over two years ago. She had even protested at the necessity of this most recent trip, though her protests had been half-hearted. Dianna was well aware of the reason for Shiye's frequent ventures, and she was very thankful for them. There was no guarantee that Shiye's people had given up searching for him.

Almost four years ago, Shiye's father had arranged for him to marry the daughter of a chief in the neighboring tribe. The two tribes had been at war for years. There was fault on both sides, and it was finally agreed that the children of the leaders would marry in order to bring peace to their people. Shiye was the son of Chief Niíchaad, who sent Shiye to live with the opposing people, and to marry Tiponi, the daughter of Chief Kuckunniwi.

Shiye had done his best to acclimate to his new surroundings, and tried to befriend the woman he was supposed to marry, but it had been difficult. Tiponi was not a kind woman. She was abrasive and cruel. Spoiled from the moment of her birth, and convinced it was her birthright, she ran the people of her tribe in circles as they attempted to do her bidding. Her father was a just man, but Tiponi was the eldest of Kuckunniwi's children and favored by him. He doted on her and easily dismissed any accusations of bullying or unkindness on her part.

Although Shiye didn't approve of the way Tiponi treated her people, he chose to honor his father's wishes. He created a mutual tolerance for the woman, who displayed her animosity towards him in the form of boasts.

"Look at our land. See how it flourishes? Your land does not thrive as ours does. Look at our warriors. They are just and right; they are powerful. Your warriors are as weak and as selfish as babes. It is good we are calling an end to the battles, for your people would not survive without ours."

One day, Tiponi brought him to the woods. Tagging along behind them was the young daughter of one of Tiponi's clansmen. Tiponi had made her come with them to carry their supplies. She brought Shiye to a river and pointed down at the water.

"The fish are so plentiful here that they leap in our nets," she said, lifting her necklace to her lips and gnawing absently on the thread that bound the beads. "We have enough to feed armies of warriors."

"That is good," Shiye said, "for together, our armies will surely be more powerful than any other." Tiponi smiled meanly at him, still chewing on her beads. Her dark hair had been loose, and she seemed to be trying to gauge Shiye's possibilities as she stared at him.

"I don't want to marry you," she said bluntly. "I think your people are weak, immoral, and filthy." Shiye rounded on her, furious, and had trouble containing his anger. "This union is for our people. It is to bring an end to the deaths that will follow if we fail. We will marry. You will be my wife."

Tiponi clutched at her beads, her eyes a little mad as she laughed. "You think so?" she said. "You think I will bow to you?"

"I am not asking you to bow," growled Shiye, and he took hold of Tiponi's arm and shook her slightly. "Our people have fought for decades. We have a chance to bring an end to the bloodshed."

Tiponi laughed again, still tugging at her beads, and the strand she had been chewing on broke in her hand. "I will bathe in the blood of your people," she said viciously, "I will revel in their decrease." She had tromped over to the young girl that had accompanied them and shoved her broken necklace into her hands. "Mend it, you useless lump," she shrieked and then she spun back to Shiye once more.

"Your people deserve your respect," he cut across her before she could speak again. " They are of you. For you. You are the same. They do not belong to you. They are not your slaves."

"I will treat my people however I wish," Tiponi shrieked, and she rounded on the little girl and shoved her off her perch and to the ground.

Shiye cried out in outrage and ran to help the child back to her feet, but she would not stir.

"What have you done?" he yelled at Tiponi as he saw the blood gushing from the place where the child had struck her head on a jagged stone behind her.

Tiponi looked horrified for a moment, but then a smile crept eerily up the corners of her mouth.

"Oh, no," she said, her eyes raking Shiye's bloodstained hands as he tried to staunch the flow. "What have you done, Shiye?"

When he next looked up, Tiponi had

disappeared.

She returned with her father and the people of the tribe a few moments later and pointed to where Shiye sat, coated in the little girl's blood.

"Look, Father. He has murdered Matchitehew's child. He tried to kill me as well!" She turned to her tribesmen, screaming over Shiye as he tried to explain. "See what a mistake it was, to think we could unify our tribes? To think that his people would be a benefit to ours? He has murdered one of our own! He has killed an innocent. He must die!"

"It was not I!" yelled Shiye again and again, but the people were frenzied by Tiponi's words, and Kuckunniwi would not listen. He ordered his men to bind Shiye's arms and they led him to be executed on a high cliff where Shiye's people would see him die. Tiponi's face shone with tears, but when Shiye called to her for help, to cease this folly, she had smiled at him from behind her father's back.

Shiye wouldn't have escaped had it not been for a disturbance caused by the tribe's medicine man, Yahto. He couldn't see what happened, but Kuckunniwi left him tied to a nearby tree and went to investigate.

The son of the medicine man had approached Shiye's guards and asked for a word with the prisoner. Shiye watched him as he spoke of righting wrongs that had been done. As the boy spoke with Shiye, he slipped a knife into his hands.

Shiye was able to use the knife to slice through his bonds. He took his guards by surprise and overpowered them, then fled back to his own people.

Shiye ran through the forest, using the nearby river to cover his tracks. He could hear the sounds of Kuckunniwii and his men pursuing him, but he didn't stop until he reached his people's land.

When his father heard what had happened, Niíchaad told Shiye that he had shamed his people by allowing the chance for peace to die. He said that Shiye must be punished for his misdeeds. Then he tied his son to a tree and whipped him until his back was raw.

Shiye's father would not shelter him within the tribe. With nowhere to go and nowhere to hide, Shiye had had no choice but to run, and keep running, for he knew that Tiponi's people would hunt him always.

That was where Dianna came in. In danger of becoming a spinster in New York, she had taken it upon herself to answer Greyson Crowley's advert in the newspaper. After only corresponding a few times, Dianna had agreed to travel to Wyoming to marry him. Her family had been very reluctant to let her go, but Dianna had followed her instincts, and insisted that her departure would be for the better. So she had gone, leaving behind her three younger sisters, her mother, and her father. It had nearly broken her heart to leave them, but Dianna could not shake the feeling that Wyoming held answers for her.

Love had found her, eventually, though not in the way she had expected. Dianna had foolishly hoped to make a new life with Greyson, who had revealed himself to be a drinking man who often became violent. Unbeknownst to Dianna, he had taken up the habit after his first wife had passed. He had scared off all but one of his ranch hands, and one night, when Dianna had been careless enough to vent her temper on the matter, he had thrown Dianna across the room, causing a gruesome head injury that might have killed her. Severely wounded and bleeding copiously, Dianna had fled into a winter's night and been rescued by Shiye. They had spent months in an earthen cave while Shiye nursed Dianna back to health. Slowly, but surely, glances became longer and attraction blossomed into love.

After a run-in with Greyson, from which they were rescued by Parker—the one and only ranch hand that had remained with Greyson after he'd developed his love of whiskey—Shiye and Dianna were married in the Spring.

They continued to run from Tiponi's tribesmen and even now, years later, Shiye would wake in the night, covered in sweat, wondering where Kuckunniwi was now. Remembering Tiponi's livid face, and her laughing, mad eyes.

Shiye only rested for two weeks before he began preparing for his trip into town. Dianna approached her husband outside the small barn as he lifted a saddle onto Tanulonli's back, feeling unaccountably nervous.

Shiye's horse was shifting its black stockinged feet, already eager to be off. He was a hulking animal, heavy-boned and sturdy, and he wore his buckskin pelt as though it were a tailored suit on a wealthy man's back. Dianna took hold of the horse's muzzle and began stroking over his velvety nose.

"You look after my husband, 'Lee," she said to it, using the nickname she had derived from his given one.

Shiye rolled his eyes at his wife. "Tanulonli," he stressed the name, "will take good care of me."

"I know he will," smiled Dianna, and she planted a kiss on the horse's nose. Tanulonli's great brown eyes stared interestedly into her own. His ears pricked forward, listening to the sound of her voice. "Perhaps we should-?"

"Wait?" Shiye cut her off. He finished tying the flap on his saddle bag closed and turned to his wife, an exasperated smile playing over his lips. "If I wait any longer the baby will be here, and we'll be running out of supplies while you're trying to heal. I have to go now. I shouldn't have waited as long as I did."

Dianna opened her mouth to protest further, but then shut it again, conceding defeat. Shiye pulled her to him and kissed her gently. "I'll be back in six days. I won't stay any longer than I have to. I'll be home before you have time to miss me."

Dianna nodded and pushed her sadness to the back of her mind. She could mope while he was away.

"I just..." she trailed off and shrugged. Smiling wistfully, she watched her husband mount his horse. Shiye bent down to cup her face in his right hand and give her a final kiss.

"I love you," he whispered, pulling away. Dianna tried not to let her eyes fill with tears, but she couldn't help it.

"I love you too," she said. Shiye's hand slipped away. He kicked the horse into motion and rode to the edge of the trees. Once there, Shiye turned and gave her a wave. Dianna waved back and watched him leave home for the second time that month, her heart heavy, wishing she could just go with him.

"It's just you and me now," she said to her belly, cupping her hands beneath it and feeling the pleasant roundness of her child through her skin. A small jab to her fingers made Dianna smile, and she turned away from the place where Shiye had vanished into the trees. She walked to the riverbank, staring out over the sparkling water. "I know he just got back," she said, wearily. "But he really does have to go. He'll be home soon. We won't even have time to miss him." Dianna repeated Shiye's words through the tears that had already begun to fall down her cheeks. She ran her fingers over her stomach as she walked along the river, and prayed for the days to pass quickly.

Chapter Two

The weather grew steadily warmer. Shiye returned from town after only five days, Samson and Tanulonli laden with clumsily wrapped packages.

"Didn't you stop to sleep at all?" queried Dianna as she gazed up at him with concern. Shiye peered at her through bleary eyes as he climbed from Tanulonli's back.

"A bit," he said, "on the horse." He gave his wife a shifty grin and a kiss to dispel her look of outrage.

Dianna trailed concernedly after Shiye as he led the animals to a stock post next to the barn and began lifting the parcels from their backs. When Dianna moved to help him, he glared at her.

"Take the small things only," he said grumpily. Dianna shook her head at his gruffness and began unloading what she could manage.

Soon, Samson and Tanulonli were safely ensconced in the large pen off the side of the barn. Shiye gave them both grateful pats and a larger serving of grain than usual. Then he threw his arm around his wife's shoulders and they headed towards the house. He kicked off his boots outside the door and clumps of mud fell from the soles as he shoved them roughly aside with his foot.

"Aargh," he groaned. Finally sinking, weak-kneed, into the closest chair.

"Everything alright in town?"

Shiye waved his hand dismissively. "As fine as it could be," he said through a wide yawn. He straightened his legs and lifted his arms over his head, giving himself over to a long stretch.

"How are you feeling?" he asked as his body grew limp once more.

"As fine as I could be," grinned Dianna. She moved forward and planted herself on her husband's lap. Shiye grinned exhaustedly up at her.

"Very fine then?" he said, giving his hips a suggestive wiggle.

Dianna chuckled and smoothed Shiye's long, raven-colored hair back from his eyes.

"Ugh," he groaned again, burying his face in her bosom. "Is it too early for a nap?"

"It's never too early for a nap," smiled Dianna. She stood, took hold of Shiye's hand, and pulled him from his chair.

The weeks crept by. Dianna's belly grew heavier and even more uncomfortable. The baby wiggled ceaselessly through the warm summer nights, making it impossible for her to sleep.

Finally, the time came.

The sun had not yet managed to scale the distant mountains when Dianna felt a painful twinge. She let out a soft "Oh," and Shiye awoke in the small bed as if her small noise had been the ringing of a church bell. He gazed blearily around the cabin, finally locating his wife amongst the early-morning shadows next to the fire.

"Are you alright?" he asked, sliding from the bed and dragging the soft quilted blanket with him.

Dianna waved her hand, which was still clasping the tiny sock she was crocheting and gave Shiye a tender smile.

"The baby was just letting me know she's excited to meet me. As if I could possibly forget," she groaned.

She let her head fall back on the rocking chair and closed her eyes. Shiye approached his exhausted wife and crouched down next to her. Dianna opened one red-rimmed eye to peer at him.

"Have you slept?"

"An hour or two," she answered, raising the back of her hand to conceal a yawn. Another sharp pain came then and Dianna winced and clutched at her stomach. Shiye's brow furrowed and he gave her a searching look.

"Have the pains been coming one after the other like this?"

"They just started," said Dianna, rubbing at a sore spot in her ribs. Shiye's eyes widened, but she reached forward and gave his hand a gentle pat. "Don't worry. It will be a long while yet."

"It sounds as though it might be time," whispered Shiye doubtfully and he cast an eye down Dianna's bulging front.

She waved her hand once more. "This will probably go on for days, darling."

Shiye raised an eyebrow as his wife let out another startled gasp. When the pain subsided, she took hold of his hand once more. "I had a friend in Manhattan who labored to have her son for five days before he was born."

Another pain twisted her insides. Shiye's gaze darkened with worry as she stood and pushed him gently out of her path. A sudden heaviness took hold of Dianna as she went to take her first step and she felt something give. Warm liquid slid down her legs and dampened the front of her night rail. Shiye shook his head at the shocked expression on her face and went to grab a towel.

"It doesn't look as though that will be the case with our child," he said, and he took hold of Dianna and guided her over to the bed.

The baby was born in a matter of hours. Dianna, her forehead beaded with sweat, held out her arms for the tiny bundle. Shiye grinned and passed his new daughter to her mother. Dianna's eyes gleamed with happy tears as she looked down at her child.
"Hello, Little Rose, what took you so long?"

......

She grew. And grew. Black tufts of hair turned into curls and waves. Days stretched into weeks. Weeks into long months. Years sped by. Dianna watched it all happen in the blink of an eye.
Rose's skin was the color of dark tea and cream, and her hair was as black as her father's. Her face was full and round-cheeked with the proud forehead that marked Shiye's ancestry. They were so alike, but around Rose's full lips and pointed noise, Dianna caught glimpses of herself and her family. Her brows were thick and dark, and her stubborn streak reminded Dianna of the trouble *she* had caused when she was young.
Standing beside one another in the bright, afternoon sunlight, Dianna observed that her husband and daughter had obviously been cut from the same cloth.
Their expressions mirrored one another as they both lifted their hands to shield their eyes from the glare of the sunlight on the river. Their noses wrinkled in identical expressions of irritation.
A fish jumped.
"There!" Rose pointed, "Did you see it, Mama?"
"I did!" shouted Dianna from her position on the front porch a few yards away. Rose's grin stretched

across her entire face. She beamed up at her father has he cast a line into the river and then sat down on the bank beside her.

Dianna watched them for a few more minutes before turning and moving back into the cool interior of the house.

Her eyes skated over the leather bags that sat, packed and ready, on the kitchen table and fell onto the small bundle of letters next to them. The six envelopes sat one on top of the other, tied with a thin black ribbon. Dianna heaved a sigh and her heels knocked against the wood floor as she moved across the room and lifted the bundle.

The handwriting on the front of the most recent envelope belonged to her mother. It was the first time she had written to Dianna in the nearly six years since she had first left Manhattan.

This fact stabbed at her insides anytime she thought about it. She loved her family very much, and it had nearly pulled her apart to leave them. She thought of them every day and had written to them as often as she could manage. The post office box in Buffalo Creek was always full to bursting with letters from her sisters.

Charlotte, who always sounded irritable, wrote to her in a matter-of-fact way. She told Dianna of the day-to-day life in the Brittler household. Of the parties and gowns, of the servant's gossip and their father's business dealings.

Sarah talked of nothing but her new husband in her letters, and of her longing to see Dianna.

Every time Dianna opened one of Sarah's letters, her heart was flooded with a sickening guilt. She had missed Sarah's wedding, and though she had managed to send her a gift—a handmade quilt, fox-fur scarf, and an intricately beaded handbag—she hated the distance between them more than she hated anything else.

Noelle was again, different. Her letters were more reserved than she had ever been when Dianna left home, and Dianna had a sense that Noelle had grown. Six years was a very long time to not see her sisters. Of course, she had never thought that it would be six years. It had never crossed her mind that her plans to marry Greyson Crowley would be thwarted by the very man himself. What had she been thinking of? Where had her good sense been? Why had her family ever let her go? Dianna asked herself these questions in the back of her mind, but couldn't ever bring herself to regret the decision she had made all those years ago. She had wanted adventure, and here it was. Stomping in the front door with giggles and a small fish on a hook.

"Look, Mama. Look what we caught!" Rose held the slick fish by its string, her hazel eyes bright with excitement. "Papa let me do it!" she said proudly.

Dianna laughed. "Very good!" she said. "So I suppose *you* will be cooking supper this evening?" Rose giggled again as Dianna took the fish from her hands, then she flew back out into the sunshine.

This was her adventure. This life she had built with Shiye. This was their happiness and their future. It would not do to dwell on the past.

Dianna pulled open the letter on the top of the stack.

Dianna,
It has been a long while since you came home. I am most concerned at the path your life has taken. An Indian man? You cannot be serious. Please tell me your sisters are lying to me.
A woman of your birth cannot possibly have

shackled herself to a savage beast of a man whom she met in a cave. Tell me this is not true.

The girls are telling me that you have a child with this man. What do you plan to do with a child that is half Indian? I hope you will school her at home, she will not be accepted to any of the finishing schools. The other children will laugh at her. If you even live in a home, that is.

This is absolutely outrageous. I'm quite ashamed of your behavior. I never brought you up to act this way. I did not raise you for a life of poverty and squalor. I demand you return home. Leave the man, bring the child. We will find something to do with her. In the meantime, we shall find you a respectable position as a governess. You must come home. I have sent you enough money to travel back to us. If you do not return, we shall send someone for you.

Mother

Dianna sighed. Her chest boiled with fury but deep down, she knew she could have expected no less from her mother. Samantha Brittler was accustomed to wealth and propriety. She had been an overbearing and strict disciplinarian, and she had never had any tolerance for anything that might bring negative attention to the family. Dianna had never seen eye to eye with the woman, but even knowing all that, she felt a certain sense of guilt at the idea that her mother did not approve of her marriage. This thought was immediately put aside. Dianna was *happy*, and she was a good wife to Shiye. A good mother to Rose. She knew the Lord would not despise her for her choice of husband, and she hoped in her heart that her mother would grow to forgive her for her making a choice that she deemed quite unsuitable.

Beneath her mother's letter was another. This one carried the heavy-handed, slanted handwriting that she knew to be her fathers. His letters had come just as frequently as her sisters' had, and though he was obviously not pleased with her circumstances, he at least, seemed to accept that it was her choice. Dianna assured him over and over again that she was happy, that they were safe, and proudly told him that Rose had inherited her grandfather's nose. She had been able to envision her father smiling when he read this.

She was happy, but she missed her family so much it felt as though she was enduring a constant stomachache. The thought of her mother's letter haunted her as she made her way out to the horses' paddock. Tawny greeted her with his usual nudge and snort of pleasure, and Dianna opened the gate to lead him over to the small barn a short distance away. The horse could tell they were readying for a journey, and he danced excitely as Dianna lifted a saddle onto his back.

"Sit still," she told him softly, smiling fondly at him. Tawny's brown eyes gazed at her reproachfully as she tightened the strap and inserted a bit into his mouth, but he calmed down and sat unnaturally still for her, his long tail swishing behind him, swatting away unwanted flies.

"Almost ready then?"

Dianna jumped at the sound of Shiye's voice behind her and then relaxed into the warmth of his embrace as his arms encircled her waist.

"Just about," she said, allowing her head to drop back onto his shoulder. "Are you ready?"

Dianna felt Shiye nod against the back of her neck, and his lips came to rest on the skin there, causing Dianna to sag in his arms. "Just about," he whispered. He nipped softly at the skin beneath his lips and then turned to pull Tanulonli from the paddock as well.

"Momma?" Rose's small hand gave her skirt a tug, and Dianna looked down into her daughter's bright, round face. "Can I bring LooLoo?"

Dianna bent and scooped Rose into her arms, eyeing the flop-eared toy rabbit she held in her chubby fists. "I don't see why not," Dianna said, taking the rabbit and twitching his ears back and forth. "It looks like he's excited to go into town."

Rose smiled and wrapped her arms around Dianna's neck, then she pulled back and frowned. "Will it be the looonng ride again?"

Dianna heard Shiye snort with amusement as he brought his horse up alongside hers. "Yes, we'll ride for a few days," she said, and then she laughed as Rose's nose wrinkled in disgust.

They brought their saddle bags outside, then Shiye gathered Rose into his arms and set her on Tawny's back. Dianna stole a kiss from her husband as he helped her up after their daughter, and they were off.

Rose turned and peered longingly over Dianna's shoulder as they slid through the trees, away from their home.

"My friend will miss me," she grouched, squeezing the saddle horn with her small, pink hands.

"Your friend?" asked Dianna indulgently, "which friend, darling?"

"His name is Chew," said Rose, sticking out her lower lip. "He's always been my friend. You can't see him."

"No, and why is that?" Dianna looked down at the top of Rose's dark-haired head, which swayed from side to side as Tawny made his way over the earth.

"He says it is because are íaxxaaxii bíhka, like a horse." Her father's people's words sounded guttural on her tiny tongue.

Dianna drew herself up, affronted. "Where did you hear such a term?"

"From Chew," said Rose matter-of-factly, shrugging her small shoulders. Dianna egged Tawny forward and brought her horse up beside Shiye's, who smiled lazily at her from beneath the brim of his hat. His dark hair flowed smoothly over the collar of his coat, and his broad shoulders were relaxed and untroubled. This changed the moment he caught sight of Dianna's expression.

"Our daughter has just told me," she said in a huff, "that she has a friend who thinks I am íaxxaaxii bíhka, like a horse." Her eyes could have thrown daggers at him, but Shiye merely shrugged.

"A very fine horse?" he suggested in his warm native-tongue, looking over the top of Rose's head at the place where Dianna's bosom wiggled with the bumpiness of the trail they rode. Dianna glared at him and he sobered. "I don't know where she heard it, Di. It certainly must have come from me, but if I said those words, it wasn't directed at you."

"If?" Dianna snapped, and she gave Tawny a sharp kick so that they drew ahead of Shiye. She could feel his eyes on her swaying figure and made sure to sit uncomfortably straight in the saddle, making her irritation with him prominent.

"I meant *when*. When I said them," he called after her retreating back.

He should be more careful around Rose, thought Dianna sniffly, *Dirty animal, indeed.*

Her bad attitude lasted all of fifteen minutes.

They came to an unkempt dirt road lined with tall spruce and turned right, heading towards town. Shiye was repentant. He cast many side-long looks at his wife, smiling sheepishly, finally drawing Tanulonli up beside them and sliding sideways in his saddle to seize Tawny's reins and tug them to a halt.

"I am sorry," he said, planting a kiss on her jaw. "I will be more careful with my words." Dianna felt her irritation with her husband ease.

"I want her to learn, but not from the irritable muttering you do when the animals are being stubborn."

"What about when my wife is being stubborn," he teased, poking her in the side. Dianna rolled her eyes and Shiye turned his attention to his daughter.

"You can't say everything your Pa says," he grumbled at her.

Rose looked defensive. "But I didn't hear it from you, Papa, I heard it from Chew," she said, folding her little arms crossly.

Shiye quirked an eyebrow questioningly at Dianna. "It's her new friend," she explained, putting heavy emphasis on the word so that he would understand that Chew only existed in their daughter's very creative mind.

"He's not new," said Rose, "he's always been there."

"Of course he has, dear," said Dianna. Rose still looked grumpy at her parent's dismissal of her friend. Her lower lip was jutting out in a full pout but she brightened again as they moved on.

They made camp that night in a small clearing. It was a clear, cool night and crickets chirped lazily around them as Dianna started the fire in one smooth strike.

Shiye smiled at her, pulling out bedrolls, pans,

and other miscellaneous items from their bags.

Rose dozed fitfully that night, her head on her father's chest, her mother cuddled closely beside her. They slept in the open, beneath the stars, and Dianna dreamed of flames.

At first, it was warm, pleasant even. They danced over her face and arms and tickled her skin like the touch of Shiye's lips, like the small palm of Little Rose's hand.

Then there came a change. She stood on the edge of a field, looking down at their home as her husband and daughter played hide and seek within the trees.

"I'm coming to get you!" said Shiye, and when he found Rose, he tickled her. Dianna smiled, her heart full of happiness and contentment.

The warmth of the fire returned. It was at her back now and Dianna spun around to see that the entire field behind her had been set ablaze. The flames were licking their way over the dry grass, gliding snake-like over the earth and creeping towards the tiny cabin and the place where her family played, unaware of the coming danger. She ran to them, but the faster she ran, the slower she went, and the faster the flames crept towards the ones she loved.

She tried to cry out a warning. Her heart was pounding in her chest; her head was fit to burst. The flames came closer, and Dianna fell to the ground, they seared up the length of her foot, and wound themselves around her ankles like fiery chains, holding her in place.

Shiye and Rose could not hear her screaming for them to run. Dianna spun, looking for the person who had set the blaze on those she loved. On the other side of the flames, across the crackling field of fire, there stood the indistinct form of a man. Dianna could only see his white teeth as he pulled them back in a satisfied smile, and then he was gone, and the flames grew tall and swallowed Dianna whole.

She was sweating when she woke. Rose's cold little fist was clamped tight around a strand of Dianna's blonde hair.

It took several long moments before she was able to quiet her racing heart. When she did, she sat up. Her daughter's hand fell into her lap, and Dianna took hold of it softly, feeling the reassuring twitch of sleepy little fingers in her palm. She leaned over and brushed a kiss over Rose's forehead, then smoothed a stray strand of dark hair from Shiye's cheek.

It was a dream, she told herself. Nothing more than that. Why then was her chest so full of tainted dread?

The taste of ash and smoke was thick on her tongue and her throat felt parched. Moving slowly, so as to not to wake them, Dianna slid herself away from Shiye and Rose's warm bodies and stood. Her body ached in protest of having slept on the hard ground, but it made Dianna smile. The discomfort reminded her of the day she and Shiye had met, of the long winter nights they had spent together in that cramped cave on the mountain.

She wandered away from their camp and crouched down next to the gently trickling stream. The refreshing taste of the water washed away all remnants of the terrifying dream she had had. It flowed through her fingers and down her throat with sweet encouragement, giving her the strength to understand the warning she had been given. Something was coming, Dianna could feel it in her bones, and it was her duty to protect her family from those that would harm them. Her fingers trembled slightly, and she glanced around the pressing darkness with a newfound fear. Who knew what may lurk in the shadows of the night? She hurried back to her place beside Rose, but she did not dare to close her eyes until the darkness began to wane.

Chapter Three

Shiye awoke, bleary-eyed and tousle-haired, and his eyes sought his wife. She was sitting bolt upright, her eyes red-rimmed and a little wild.

"What is the matter?" he asked quietly. Careful not to wake Rose, who snored gently next to him. Shiye reached out a placatory hand to clasp her soft fingers. Dianna started a little at the sound of his voice, and her bloodshot eyes flew to him, their blue alarmingly stark in the muted morning light.

She gave him a tremulous smile. "I had a nightmare," she whispered. The warm air surrounding her words flooded from her pale lips in a cloud of white mist.

"Oh, darling," Shiye said and he gestured her over to them. She came, tired and wan and shivering slightly. He tugged her close to him and Rose and his eyes took in the fear in hers. He threw a warm fur over her shoulders and began to rub them vigorously, remembering how he had done so all those years ago, remembering the jolt he had felt at her first smile, her first laugh in his presence. He had known then, that he wanted her for his own, but never in his wildest dreams had he believed she would ever be his, let alone give him a beautiful child who looked so very like him.

Shiye cupped his wife's cold cheeks in his warm palms and kissed her frozen lips. She smiled at him. He felt the familiar thrill of pleasure, of wanting, and he bent over Rose's small form to kiss Dianna again. She tasted of honey and of roses. An intoxicating combination that he wanted to feel on his lips over and over until she was the only thing he could taste, until the very breath in his lungs was filled with her sweetness, but he desisted in favor of offering her comfort.

"Tell I," he said to her, which made her smile. It was a joke. When Shiye and Dianna had first met, his English had comprised some twenty-odd words, five of which he had been unable to pronounce correctly. Six years passed and he still had difficulty on rare occasions, but this was not one of those times. Dianna had been very patient in teaching him, but in the beginning, his misplacement of the words 'me' and 'I' had been quite frequent. Along with innumerable other mistakes.

Still smiling at him, Dianna shook her head. "It's over now," she whispered, tugging herself closer to him and firmly sandwiching their daughter between them. Rose shifted irritably but didn't wake, and Dianna slid her icy fingers into his shirt, making him shiver and causing his skin to break out in gooseflesh. He winced as her hands sought the warmest places on his body, and his wife chuckled naughtily.

"You're making me cold all over," he hissed at her, fighting to tug his shirt back into place without waking their daughter. But Dianna had settled now, her clammy fingers planted firmly in the hot space between his forearm and his ribs, and her trembling was slowing.

Shiye reached out and wedged his family into his arms. Brushing golden hair away from her bright blue gaze, he kissed Dianna one last time and urged her back to sleep. The sun had not yet risen, the morning was still dim, and she obviously needed the rest. Another few hours and they would rise together and continue along the path.

They reached the small town of Buffalo Creek two days later. Rose was chatting enthusiastically, asking to visit her favorite shops. There was a friendly man who owned a supply store just up the road. He always had a candy for Rose, and she was bubbly and excited now that they had finally arrived at their destination.

"... And, Mama, could I have a new dress?" Shiye felt Dianna's gaze on him questioningly and he looked up from the place where he was busily counting their money and goods to trade. Rose's eager smile would have melted any heart that happened to pass by, but he didn't want to get her too excited.

"We'll have to get everything else first," he said absently to her, his eyes returning to his task, "and then we shall see."

Rose squealed with excitement. Shiye rolled his eyes and shook his head.

They had climbed off their horses next to the post office and tied them to the hitch there.

"Stay out here with Papa," said Dianna. The postmaster in Buffalo Creek was notoriously bad tempered. Shiye recalled, with a rush of pleasure, the absurdly amiable Warren Bram. The postmaster in Cheyenne, several hundreds of miles away. How he wished he could thank the man. He wanted to tell Warren how much his kindness had meant to him the day they had met. Warren had not even acted as though he noticed Shiye's dark skin. He had welcomed him into his office and proved to Shiye that there was more goodness amongst Dianna's people than he had initially given them credit for. As if Dianna hadn't been proof enough.

Rose skipped happily around his feet, tugging at his shirt and jabbering rapidly.

"Aí Rose," he said exasperatedly, taking hold of her little arm as she made to dart around him again, "settle yourself down."

She quieted respectfully and remained subdued until her mother walked back out of the post office a few moments later.

"We should start at the supply store," he said without looking up, "we need to—" he broke off. He had only just caught sight of his wife's face. Her cheeks had drained of blood, she looked ghostly, standing there in the autumn sunlight, her golden hair blowing eerily around her face and her eyes still puffy from her repeated lack of sleep on their journey.

"I have to go," she said.

Shiye frowned at her, these words taking an inordinate amount of time to penetrate his preoccupation about the supply store.

"What?" he said, looking from her to the open letter in her hand confusedly.

"I have to go home," she almost whispered. She was biting on her lower lip, always a danger sign.

"We won't be in town very long," said Shiye puzzled, coming over to get a closer look at Dianna's pallid expression. She didn't seem to hear him.

"My father. He's ill. Deathly ill. I have to go," she held out the letter in her hand. Shiye didn't take it. It seemed his wife had forgotten that he couldn't read very well.

"What does it say?"

Dianna seemed to come back to herself a little. She withdrew the hand holding the letter and her fingers shook slightly as she brought it up to her eyes to read it aloud.

Dianna,

Head for home. Father has fallen ill. We fear his battle might be at an end any day. Come home.

Sarah

Tears filled Dianna's eyes. "I have to go," she said again, and she stepped towards Rose and lifted her onto Tawny's back. "Today. Now." She reached out and took Shiye's hand, her cold fingers wrapped momentarily around his warm ones. Their extreme temperatures combined. He felt the heat that had crept into his veins disintegrate at her touch.

He nodded.

"Let's go."

They used the money and trades they had brought to barter for enough supplies to sustain them on the ride to Hunton's Ranch. The journey would be long, but it was the closest town with a train station.

Every time Shiye looked at his wife, he willed them to sprout wings. To fly to the place she so desperately longed to be. He prayed that her father would be there when they arrived. His heart ached for her.

She was cool and sturdy, preparing everything they would need with a meticulous detachment that bordered on indifference. She was sharp, and her tongue bit at those that impeded their progress. The owner of the supply store acted slightly offended by her forwardness as she entered the store and approached the counter with enough purpose that she parted the few people gathered there as though she were the man, Moses, from her bible stories, the one who parted the sea.

Shiye stepped in front of Dianna as she went to address the owner.

"We're in a bit of a hurry, Gerald," he said by way of a greeting and an apology. He could feel Dianna seething as she side-stepped him and he took hold of her arm to stop her from making a scene. He shot her a warning look, and, though her shoulders stiffened with indignation, he saw her brow relax slightly. She took hold of Rose's hand and turned to prowl the shelves like a lioness.

"Her father has fallen ill," he said in an undertone.

Gerald nodded his head. He was a tall, portly man in a plain white button-up with a black apron over the front of it. "I've never seen her so riled up," he said. "Looked like she was 'bout ready to spring at me."

"My apologies," said Shiye.

"No need," said Gerald, waving an airy hand the size of a shovel spade. "What can I get around for you?"

Shiye handed him a small list. "You been into Hunton's Ranch, lately?"

"Not for a long while. Usually go into Chugwater if I need anything particular." Gerald slid a pair of thick spectacles onto the end of his nose to look at the list Shiye had handed him and then stared over the top of them as Dianna set a wooden crate of various odd and ends onto the counter.

"This too," she said curtly. Shiye raised his eyebrows at her. "Please," she corrected herself.

Gerald smiled and gave her hand a pat. "We'll have you heading off just as soon as we can, Miss D."

Dianna forced a smile. Shiye's hand found hers beneath the counter.

"Patience," he whispered in her ear, "we'll get there."

Half an hour later Shiye was loading their parcels onto Tanulonli's back. He hefted a package of food and slid it into the rest of the supplies, then clasped the large bag and turned to shake Gerald's hand. Dianna was already lifting Rose, who'd been remarkably quiet throughout the whole ordeal, onto her horse's back.

"We're not going home, are we, Mama?" Rose looked close to tears.

Dianna hoisted herself up onto the saddle behind her and turned their daughter around so that she could peer into her small, round face. "My Papa is sick," Shiye heard her whisper, "I need to go to him as quick as I can. And just think, darling, you will get to meet your aunties."

Rose's responding smile was timid. "Auntie Sarah?" she asked hopefully. "And Noelle and Charlotte too?"

"Yes, dear." Dianna bent down and planted her lips on their daughter's cheek.

Shiye was so focused on his wife's intensity he was hardly listening to what Gerald was saying to him about the passes through the Black Hills.

"Might have to skirt around them if there's snow on the ground 'round the time you hit Laramie Peak."

"We'll do that," said Shiye, coming back to the conversation and mentally cataloging the information before it could slip away. "Laramie Peak, you say?"

"That's right. If there's snow on the ground right there. Head around the long way, because the pass'll be clogged up with it by the time you get to the top."

Shiye nodded. "Thanks very much, Gerry. I'll be seeing you."

"Yeah, in a year or two," chuckled the beefy man. "Safe trip."

Shiye tipped his hat to Gerald and climbed onto Tanulonli's back. He heard Rose's small voice echoing back as they moved out.

"Thank you for the candies Mr. Gerry, sir!"

Gerald waved and smiled. Shiye tipped his hat to him and glanced over his shoulder at his wife. Her eyes were full of a steely determination that he'd only seen in them a handful of times. The first time had been a long while ago now, but he could still remember it as clear as day.

The breeze had blown through her golden hair on the top of a hillside overlooking Fort Russel and she had been fierce in her proclamation.

"I will follow you if you go," she had whispered and though her voice had been soft, it had carried a threat. "I will chase you more surely than those that hunt you. I will hunt you, and they will hunt me. Let me stay by your side. I never want to be anywhere else."

Shiye's hands tightened on the reins in front of him. Wherever Dianna wanted to be, that was where he would be also. That was how they worked. They followed one another over the valleys and hillsides, across mountains. Into the darkest, deepest valleys of the Earth, he would follow his beloved. And deeper still. *Wherever* she wanted to be, that's where he would be also.

"Ya!" he shouted as they reached the edge of Buffalo Creek. He heard Dianna's voice shout the same and they were off.

He knew what he was heading towards as his horse's hooves pounded away the miles between his wife's family and his home. He knew he was heading to shame, to ridicule, far away from the happy life he had built with his family, but he knew too that Dianna would stand firm by his side. She wouldn't shrink from him. Her people would. Her family would, but Dianna never had. She was not ashamed of their love or their life together. She had never seen him as a beast but as a man. Her man.

He wasn't scared, but he couldn't deny his apprehension. Manhattan was a far cry from Wyoming, where dark skin wasn't exactly welcome, but at least heard of and acknowledged. In Manhattan, people would run from him in the streets. He glowered at the trees that flashed by. He'd be lucky not to be burned at the stake.

Chapter Four

It took three days for them to reach Laramie Peak, and to his relief, there wasn't a patch of snow to be seen.

"Up and over the hills then," he said firmly. Dianna nodded as Tawny snorted and danced. Rose had fallen asleep in her mother's arms. Her small eyes were ringed in shadows. None of them were sleeping very well on the ground at night, and the November weather was bitingly cold.

They climbed the Black Hills, heading for Hunton's Ranch and the closest train station. The train would take them South to Cheyenne, and then East, on to Manhattan, with frequent stops along the way.

Shiye's eyes were heavy too, only Dianna looked fully functional. Her concern for her father had evidently given her an endurance that he lacked. He was tired. His backside ached from its prolonged contact with Tanulonli's saddle and he wanted nothing more than to crawl into a warm bed and sleep for a decade.

The mountain air nipped at the exposed skin of their cheeks and noses, and he was relieved when they finally stood at the foot of the hills where the air was warmer.

Dianna pulled down the kerchief she had tied around her face to reveal teeth that chattered slightly and cheeks so pink she looked as though she had rouged them.

"Should we camp here? Or seek somewhere more sheltered?"

"More sheltered, I think," said Shiye, eyeing the huddled lump in his wife's arms that was their sleeping daughter.

They made camp in a small clearing. Large boulders littered the surrounding trees, casting vast shadows in the darkening light. They ate in shivering silence around a large fire, their backs against one of the largest boulders. With the rock at their back and the fire at their front, the night felt warmer than it had in a long while. It was with relief that Shiye curled his wife and daughter into his arms and laid his head down to rest for the night.

He awoke much earlier than he would have liked, alert and wary, ears pricking at the sound of harsh whispers from the trees. Terror gripped him, and he launched himself to his feet as he realized that Rose's small, warm body was no longer beside his.

"Rose?!" he called out into the night. He spotted her a few moments later, her brown dress and dark hair nearly blending perfectly with the encompassing shadows of the timber. He darted to her side and grabbed her arm. "What're you doing?" he said. He lifted her, and she wrapped freezing arms around his wide shoulders.

"I was talking to Chew," she said through chattering teeth. Shiye rolled his eyes.

"Chew needs to go to bed," he said irritatedly, "and you know better than to wander off in the night. You might get hurt out there all alone."

"But I wasn't alone, Papa," chattered Rose, burying the cold tip of her nose in the flesh of his neck and making him wince. "Chew was—"

"I think Chew needs to respect your Father's words just as much as you do. Don't you dare wander off into the night on your own, do you understand?"

He felt Rose's small chest heave a great sigh against his own. "Yes, Papa," she said.

His heart calmed. "It's dangerous," he whispered, depositing his daughter next to Dianna, who had sat up worriedly, clutching blankets of fur to her chest.

"What were you doing, Little Rose?" she quizzed, opening her arms and tucking Rose to her bosom.

"She was speaking with Chew again," answered Shiye grumpily.

"In the dead of night?" Shiye saw Dianna's eyes dart all around them in the dark. The fire had nearly burned itself out, and Shiye got up to stoke it.

"He told me he was happy to have found me," said Rose, her eyes following her father's movements. "He said he had been worried when we did not return from town."

"Well," muttered Dianna, her fear apparently abating in favor of a reprimand. "It is very kind of Chew to have come all this way to see you, but I do think he should wait until the morning to wake you."

"He cannot come out when you are awake," said Rose simply, shrugging her little shoulders. Shiye caught Dianna's eye and they exchanged a grin.

"Of course he can't, dear," whispered Dianna. Shiye watched her draw Rose closer to her soft body and snuggle down in their bedding. "But if you leave your bed in the night again, your father will have to give your rump a good swatting."

"I'm sorry, Mama," squeaked Rose and Dianna frowned at her. "Let's not have there be a next time." Rose shook her little head violently and Shiye ruffled her dark locks as he climbed back into bed.

"You know you're to wake your Mother if you need to get up in the night, so you best do it," he said.

Then he kissed his girls' heads, tucked his family back under his chin, and closed his eyes once more.

They arrived in Hunton's Ranch a day and a half later and rode straight to the train station to check the schedule. Dianna looked relieved when she returned to them.

"There's a train to Cheyenne arriving tomorrow afternoon. I bought three tickets."

Shiye nodded, trying not to notice the way the townspeople stared at them as they passed.

"Let's find somewhere to rest for the night."

They boarded the train early and made their way to the back of the car, drawing all eyes onto them as they passed. Rose was energetic. They had had their first good night's sleep in several days while staying in the barn of a local blacksmith for the night. It was clear they had all needed it. Shiye's temper was not to be tested, though. He was uneasy enough in the small crowd of onlookers without drawing extra attention onto them. They had paid the blacksmith to look after their horses until they returned, with a Shiye's assurances that the animals could be sold if they didn't return before the New Year.

"Aí, calm down," he said, pulling his daughter onto his lap. Dianna glanced at him, then reached across the seat to take hold of his hand. The conductor that passed them gave them a look of the utmost disgust and Shiye had to exercise a lot of control not to ask the paunchy man if he would like Shiye to find a new location for his eyeballs. Swallowing the urge, he smiled grimly at his beautiful wife and sat back in his seat. Dianna looked lovely this morning. Her freckles were standing out particularly clearly on her pale cheeks and her golden hair was pulled back from her face, falling in loose waves down her back.

"Tell me a story?" asked Rose, turning her cheek to Shiye's chest, oblivious to the negative attention surrounding them. She looked up at him through her long, dark lashes as the train gave a small jerk. Bright sunlight from the window illuminated her round, rosy cheeks and he smiled down at her patiently.

"Wait until we've begun to move, Aí, then we can settle in for the journey." He moved her to the seat beside the window and stood up, head and shoulders towering above the rest of the men in the compartment. He bent to reach for their luggage stored below the seats. His back popped unpleasantly and he cursed softly in his native tongue. Dianna cast him a reproving look and he shot her an irritable grimace before he straightened up. Her face softened, and for a moment, Shiye could glimpse the fear and pain behind her eyes. This was a part of her he had seen little of since they'd married six years ago. She spoke of her family often, but feared for them? She'd never had a cause. He knew that her sisters were well off, married to men of fine form and finance and that her father was the owner of Brittler Steel, a factory that manufactured the steel rails being laid down across America to make travel by train feasible for many who never thought it possible. They had money—luxury even—and at times it still baffled him that his wife had left it all behind to come to the wilderness of Wyoming; to marry a man she'd never even met. But if he understood one thing about Dianna, it was her love for the country they were leaving behind today.

They lived in this Earth, at one with it. They were part of it. It was their home, the place they belonged. This drew them together. This unidentifiable need to belong to a place so wild. It was in their hearts, Wyoming bound their souls.

Chapter Five

Dianna watched Shiye's look of apprehension with a mixed feeling pity and guilt.

"You don't have to come with me," she whispered, reaching out to feel his hand in hers. The small, dark hair on the back of his knuckles tickled her palm. "You could stay and wait with Rose."

Shiye brought her pale hand up to his lips and looked deep into her eyes. "You are mine," he whispered against her fingertips. "You are a piece of me that I am not whole without. When you worry, I worry. Wherever ever you go, I go too." He kissed her hand and then came to sit beside her on the bench, their backs to the many eyes that constantly flickered in their direction.

Rose was sitting opposite them, her small eyes fixed on a point outside the window. She gave a small wave as the train gave another jerk and began to roll forward,

"Goodbye, Chew," she whispered, smiling sadly. "I shall see you when I return." Dianna's thin smile sagged at the corners as she watched her daughter bid farewell to her invisible friend.

"Can't Chew come with us?" she asked, leaning forward to look out the small window with Rose.

Her heart stopped. There was a *man* standing there, waving at her daughter through the rippled glass.

He was tall, a broad-brimmed hat pulled low over his face and a black kerchief tied around his neck.

He wore a dark, oil-slicked duster and grinned broadly at the look of terror on Dianna's face. He was sliding out of view as the train pulled out of the station, gathering speed.

"Rose, who was that?" cried Dianna, grabbing hold of her daughter's hand and pulling her away from the window. "Who is that man?"

Rose looked frightened by Dianna's sudden look of fury. Shiye was on full alert. He stepped over Dianna's skirts and peered out the window at the station in the distance, but it was now too far away to make out.

"What is it, Di?" he asked, only his eyes betrayed the same fear Dianna felt burgeoning in her chest.

"She was waving at an Indian man on the platform," Dianna could hardly breathe. "He was there. Feet away from her, smiling as we pulled away." She could feel the panic, feel herself losing control. She clutched her daughter to her chest for a moment and then took her by the shoulders and looked down into Rose's innocent face.

"It was only Chew, Mama," she whispered, her dark brows creasing in confusion. "He's always been with me. He was so sad that I was going away that he came to see me before we left."

"Dianna," said Shiye, taking hold of her arm and glancing around the compartment. Dianna looked too. They were making a scene. Eyes were glaring at her all down the train, women whispering behind their fans. She sat up straight and met every furious stare. Held their insolent gazes one by one until each of them turned away again.

"Dianna," Shiye said again. He let go of her arm and sat down beside her once more. "I'm sure it was just a coincidence. Look at our girl," he said, inclining his head in Rose's direction. "Any man would know she wasn't fully English. He probably just noticed her skin and gave her a smile."

Dianna couldn't rid herself of the image of the man's face, watching her expression of frank curiosity transform into horror. His grin had widened. He knew she had seen him. He'd wanted her to see him.

"No, Shiye. No. They've found us. They're coming after us," hissed Dianna. She batted impatiently at his hands as he went to rub her own, trying to assuage her fears. "Rose. That was Chew? Does Chew always look the same?"

Rose cocked her head to the side, making her look as though her shining, dark hair was weighing her down. "Of course. He always looks the same, Mama. People's faces don't change. He's not like you and Papa," she added cheerfully. "He has wrinkles like Gerald from the store in town."

Dianna raised her wide-eyed gaze to her husband, who, she was pleased to see, looked disturbed as well.

"If it was Matchitehew," he whispered, "we can't go back." Dianna held in a sob. Their home. Their beautiful home by the river. The mountains growing tall and strong in the distance. They would never find somewhere so wonderful for a second time. They would run, they would hide, and they would spend the rest of their lives looking over their shoulders for the men that hunted them.

Dianna sat up, bracing her back against the hard wood of the train bench and took a deep breath.

"How could we have been so blind?" she whispered to Shiye. Goosebumps erupted on her flesh, creeping up her arms and searing her insides with repugnance. *He's always been there,* Rose had said. *He's always been there.*

The man had been playing with their daughter, befriending her. What if...? He could have killed her. At any time. He could have stolen Rose from them and slit her throat in a second. Dianna's horrified eyes found Shiye's and she knew he was thinking the same thoughts. Shiye bent down and took hold of Rose's face. She looked up at him from beneath her bonnet, her hazel eyes, so very like his, filled with tears as he spoke.

"Listen to me, Little Rose," he said. "Chew is a bad man. A very bad man. You will never speak to him again. If you see him, you must scream or he will kill you."

Rose opened her mouth to argue, but Dianna stopped her. "Listen to your Papa. There has never been another who is more dangerous to you." Rose closed her mouth. Tears flowed thick and fast down her round cheeks. Dianna pulled her daughter onto her lap and held her fast.

"We could have lost her," she whispered to Shiye, rocking back and forth. Her eyes burned and she began to weep. "How could we have been so blind?" she asked again. Shiye looked wretched. He wrapped his arms around them both and Dianna could feel his fury building within him. Lord, please don't let anyone cross him on our way to Manhattan, she prayed. Don't let anyone give him a reason to vent his anger. Lord, please. Protect us. Watch over our Little Rose and thank you, thank you for saving her. She wept until she had no tears left in her body and then she sat in a numb stupor, unable to make any sense out of her thoughts.

Chapter Six

It took them a week to reach Manhattan. At every stop, every stall and every slowing of the gears, Dianna felt the anxiety rise up her chest and into her throat. She would only calm when they regained their average speed, which was not nearly fast enough. She was sick with fear. Fear at how close her daughter had come to being taken from them, and fear that her father would be gone before she could reach him. Faces swam before her eyes in the monotony of the journey. Her father. Her husband. Little Rose. The face of the man she knew still stalked them. He'd been so close. Too close.

They should never have stayed in Wyoming. They should have left the land far behind them. But they'd been so sure they were safe... Now they were safe. Dianna breathed a little easier with each passing day, with each mile. She was leaving Wyoming. They were never going back, and Matchitehew surely would not follow them that far away from his people. Not to Manhattan. Perhaps, when they arrived, they would stay.

The city glimmered at them through the smog and fumes of a gray October morning as the train wound closer to their destination. Towering, nondescript buildings housed thousands of people who simply did not know anything better. Dianna felt a stab of pity for them. Those stuffy, closeted people, living so close to one another that they hardly had room to breathe. They would never know the freedom she did.

What it felt like to watch the sway of the plains, or to inhale fresh, mountain air.

She could already smell the sickening stench of the factory vapors. It clouded her thoughts, causing dread to leak into her veins. She had run from this. The noise, and the bustle, and the smoke. She had left it all behind. Now she was returning, and if she listened closely over the sound of the grinding gears of the train car, she could almost hear the thin, melancholy factory whistles echoing over the city.

A large, enclosed platform welcomed them with the sound of pattering rain.

Dianna lifted Rose down the car steps, looking around, awash in memories. The train station looked different, as though it had matured in the six years since her departure. A fresh coat of white paint had been applied on the woodwork and the newly added covering overhead gave limited protection from the onslaught of the pouring rain. Forked lightning shattered the charcoal gray sky as Shiye followed them down the stairs, hauling their luggage, and looking put upon.

His long, leather duster swept the top of the platform, the collar pulled high on his neck to deflect some of the bitter cold. He'd tucked his long hair into a leather tie to keep it from flying into his face, but it wasn't doing much good. Even with the added protection of his wide-brimmed hat, dark strands danced over his eyes. He swiped at them irritably.

Dianna took hold of his arm, shouting over the pounding of the rain.

"I can hail a cart!" she said, and Shiye nodded and set their belongings down beneath the platform cover.

Dianna stepped carefully down the platform and looked around the empty street. Not a cart in sight. She sighed, craning her neck, and Shiye joined her a few moments later, leading a grumpy looking Rose by the hand.

"We can walk?" he said doubtfully, eyeing the growing puddles on the cobblestone path to their left.

They did. It was a revolting chore, and by the time the little family arrived at the gate of the Brittler Family estate, they were all soaked to the bone, their teeth chattering with cold. Dianna stopped in front of her parent's home and allowed herself a moment to gaze up at the towering oak in the front garden. An ancient rope swing hung by her father, Thomas Brittler, was twisting madly in the rain. It swayed with the heaving branches of the tree. The sight brought tears to her eyes. It felt as though a shadow had settled over the house before them, whispering of trials to come. Dianna shivered.

She glanced at the wide front door. The windows on either side of it were dark.

Her father had purchased the house in 1856, just before Dianna was born. It was a vast confection of the most fashionable architecture of the time. In the winter, with a coating of snow, it looked like an iced gingerbread castle. Meticulously maintained by a series of gardeners and handymen, it was painted a light blue and white. The trim and porch rails stood out starkly in the grim gray of the horrid weather.

What awaited them in there? Were they too late? Had her father already passed on from this world?

She straightened her shoulders. No, she thought. Her father was in that huge, dark house. So were her mother and sisters. Suddenly, though, after longing to see them every day for six years, she balked. Would they hate her for leaving them? And what of Shiye and Rose? She had no doubt her sisters would treat her husband and daughter with kindness, but her mother?

She recalled, with painful clarity as the wind and rain buffeted her this way and that, the words her mother had written to her just weeks ago.

"A woman of your birth cannot possibly have shackled herself to a savage beast of a man whom she met in a cave.

"The girls are telling me you have a child with this man. What do you plan to do with a child that is half Indian?"

Dianna looked down at beautiful Little Rose, who stood shivering in the cold and pulling slightly on her mother's arm.

"Please, Mama, can't we go inside? My toes are frozen."

This exhausted little plea from her daughter's pale lips jerked her back to the present. Shiye had laid a gentle hand on the small of her back and as she looked up at him, he offered her a grim smile. He looked quite extraordinarily out of place. His rain-slicked coat and dark skin made him look devilishly handsome against the backdrop of prim and proper landscaping around the yard.

Dianna smiled back hesitantly.

"I want to apologize in advance for my family's-"

Shiye held up a hand with a frown. "You are all I care about. Only you. I don't care about the treatment I received while we are here. I want you to be with your family in this time of difficulty."

"My family is here," she whispered, reaching for his hand and casting a tender look between him and Rose.

"I know," said Shiye, and he pushed open the front gate.

Dianna allowed Rose ring the front bell. It jangled through the vast house, and she pulled her daughter close to her with a reassuring smile, wrapping her hands around her shoulders and wiping a smudge of dirt off her face. Shiye stood just behind her on the front stoop. His presence a reassuring warmth at her back.

Dianna could make out indistinguishable shapes through the stained glass window on right side of the front door. The blurred outline of a dark-haired man appeared suddenly in the foyer and grew larger as it approached.

Dianna held her breath. The door was pulled open, and a stranger gazed out at her, a look of utter confusion on his face. He was a good-looking man, tall and broad-shouldered with a blue shadow of stubble on his chin. He wore a brown vest over white shirt sleeves and he looked exhausted.

"We don't have anything for you," he said grumpily after gazing at them for a moment. Dianna frowned and opened her mouth to speak, but a shout from the floor above made both of them look around.

"Dianna?! Di, is that you?!" A red-haired blur of a woman in a crisp purple dress flew down the staircase on their left. In an instant, she had shoved aside the man in the doorway and flung herself onto Dianna with enough force to nearly knock her and Little Rose flat on the ground.

"L-Lottie?" stuttered Dianna, regaining her balance and pushing her sister far enough away from her to scoot Rose out from beneath the tangle of skirts and chaos. Then she held Charlotte at arm's length so that she could get a good look at her.

Charlotte looked older, naturally. Her frizzy, red hair had smoothed down into long, luscious curls that flowed down her back in neat spirals. She was just as freckly as Dianna, and her wide, blue eyes shone brightly with unshed tears. She was beautiful and curvaceous, her face one that should be splashed on beauty advertisements in the newspaper.

She wore a purple dress of thick satin with black ruffles on the shoulders and her full lips were pulled wide in a gracious smile. She took in Dianna's bedraggled appearance with raised eyebrows and an expression of satiation, then yanked her back to her curvy bosom.

"It's you," she said, breathing hard, "you've come home."

It was a few moments before Charlotte and Dianna released one another, but when they did, both of their eyes were wet. Dianna cleared her throat.

"Lottie, this is my husband, Shiye, and my daughter, Rose."

Charlotte's eyes widened as they fell on Shiye and she stared at him for a long moment before seeming to remember her manners.

"Shiye," she said warmly, striding forward and wringing his hand in an affectionate sort of way. "It's wonderful to finally meet you."

Shiye's wary expression relaxed into a relieved smile, and he nudged Rose forward.

"I've heard much about you and your sisters from Dianna," said Shiye. "Rose, say hello to your Aunt Charlotte."

"Hello," whispered Rose shyly. She crept forward and took hold of Dianna's long brown skirt, looking up at Charlotte around the hem with shy curiosity. Charlotte crouched down on the ground so that she was on a level with Rose and stuck out her hand. Rose took it hesitantly with a glance at Dianna and then said, with her customary bluntness. "Your hair is red and you have freckles like Mama."

Charlotte laughed. "I am so delighted to meet you, Rose."

Rose frowned and reached forward to pick at a strand of her auntie's hair. "I've never seen hair this color before," she said. "You are very pretty."

Dianna beamed at her.

The man in the doorway was looking uncomfortable. "I owe you an apology," he said, sticking out his hand to Dianna. "I didn't realize who you were."

"Most understandable," said Dianna, taking his proffered hand.

"My name is Kenneth Black." His handsome cheeks were flushed with embarrassment.

"Oh," said Dianna, recalling Noelle's most recent letter to her. "You're Noelle's husband."

"That I am," he said with a grim smile. "Though she might not want to keep me after I tried to turn her eldest sister out into a storm."

Dianna laughed, and Shiye stepped forward boldly, offering his hand to Kenneth.

"I'm Dianna's husband," he said, shifting their luggage into one hand. "Good to meet you."

Kenneth didn't hesitate, but took Shiye's hand and shook it vigorously. "And you as well," he said. Dianna took a liking to him instantly. "Let's get in out of the cold."

"How is he?" Dianna asked Charlotte as they stepped over the threshold and deposited their luggage in the foyer. "Can I see him?"

Charlotte's smile slipped a little. "Father's upstairs in the library."

"What's wrong with him?" asked Dianna, her eyes darting towards the staircase. She began to make her way towards it.

"The doctor says it's his heart. He's been under a lot of strain recently." Dianna couldn't help notice to the guilty sheen that lit on Charlotte's brow.

"What's been happening, Charlotte?"

Charlotte was suddenly looking close to tears.

"I'll explain in a moment," she said, and she hurried alongside Dianna as they climbed the stairs. "He'll want to see you right away."

They reached the upper floor a second later. Charlotte led her sister down a long hallway, and Dianna felt as though she had stepped back in time. She caught brief glimpses of the rooms beyond the open doors that they passed and felt a hollow pang in the pit of her stomach. She'd grown up in this house. Hanging on the walls was evidence of her youth. A photograph of her and her parents when she was an infant, then a second, again of Dianna and her parents, this time with the edition of a chubby bundle of smiles that was Sarah-Jane on her mother's lap. There was a new picture for each of the girls, each almost a year old, a family photo with a new edition. This was how the Brittler family had grown.

Dianna drew to a halt just outside the door to the library and stared at the final picture there. It was a photograph of Sarah-Jane and her very charming husband on their wedding day. Each was beaming. The sight brought tears to Dianna's eyes. She had missed so much.

Yes, she was happy. Content with her life in Wyoming. Even now, she ached to see the sprawling countryside, the snow-capped mountains. The thought of never returning made her feel as though a shard of glass had pierced her soul. But... was it worth being so far away from her younger sisters? Away from her father when he needed her most? She would not change the fact that she had left. Not for anything. Because without her leaving, she wouldn't have Shiye, and she certainly wouldn't have Little Rose. But being back in her childhood home had made her understand something. Her family still needed her and she'd been utterly selfish to abandon them the way she had.

Charlotte had paused at the library door and looked back to see where Dianna had got to. "Di?" she called. Dianna jolted back to the present, looked around, and rushed forward. Charlotte took her by the hand and pushed open the door.

At first, Dianna could make out very little in the gloom. The only light came from the dancing flames of the flickering fire. Then there came a shriek from the corner and she was being buffeted by flailing arms as her sisters hit her and wrapped their arms around her so tightly she thought her head would burst.

Dianna didn't care. It was bliss, panicked bliss. After a few moments, she gently tugged Sarah and Noelle's arms off of her. They both had tears in their eyes.

"You came home," said Sarah, wiping at her cheeks, and staring at Dianna with wide eyes. Noelle's mouth was agape. Dianna nodded, her vision blurry, and looked over their heads to the armchair in the far corner.

Thomas Brittler had been the picture of health when Dianna had left home six years ago; a little blustery and a bit comfortable in his ways, but essentially good-natured and spry. Now he looked older than Dianna had ever seen him. His face had grown lined and his eyelids were heavy with exhaustion.

Once, he had been a well-muscled and lean man. His spectacular mustache had shone with a vitality that most men of his age had long-since lost, and his sharp eyes had gleamed with playfulness and mirth. But his black hair was peppered with white now, and he was hunched in his chair. The sparkle in his eyes seemed to have gone out.

"Di?" he whispered, and he lifted a trembling hand, stretching it out to her, though she was still ten feet away. Dianna crossed the distance to him in three strides, taking hold of his cold fingers and pressing a kiss to his knuckles.

"I'm so sorry, Father." Dianna knelt on the floor at her father's feet slippered feet, holding his hand between her own. "I'm so sorry it took me so long to reach you."

He was looking into her face. "You've changed so much," he said. His voice was hoarse and worn. He looked as though he had been drained of blood, so pale was his skin. It felt papery thin beneath Dianna's palm. "You've become a woman."

"I'm a mother now, Father," said Dianna, and she pressed his cold fingers to her cheek, trying desperately to warm them. "Your granddaughter is downstairs with her father. She wants to meet you."

"I want to see her," he said with a pained smiled. "Why isn't she with you?"

"I was in rather a hurry," said Dianna, her lips quirking up in a fretful grin as her eyes took in his thin face.

The firelight danced over his eyes, so very like hers. Thomas Brittler gave his eldest daughter's fingers another feeble squeeze and then he chuckled dryly.

"There's no need to look so worried, my dear. I'll be up and about in a very short time, I think." Dianna rolled her eyes. She couldn't help it. It was so like her father to attempt to pacify her fears. He had always tried to do so. No matter what that fear may be. A creature of the darkness? It was merely a trick of the light. Grandmama had passed? She was waiting for them in heaven. He'd broken his ribs in a tumble from his prize stallion? Certainly, not. He had only decided to take a well-deserved break from riding for a time.

No matter if his sides ached when she hugged him. No matter if lifting Charlotte onto his shoulders was against the doctor's orders. Thomas Brittler was a stubborn man with a stubborn heart. He loved fiercely. He protected his family and Lord help any man or beast that tried to make his daughters cry.

A hand came down on Dianna's shoulder as she crouched beside her father's chair. Charlotte was looking towards the door as Shiye ducked his head to enter the library, clutching Rose's hand and looking peculiarly confident as he glanced around the room. Catching sight of his wife, he side-stepped around the small crowd gathered in the doorway and made his way over to her.

Rose clung to her father's hand, her expression a mixture of unease and curiosity as she peered around his powerfully built thighs.

"Shiye," said Thomas Brittler, releasing Dianna's hand and extending his thick fingers to the hulking Indian man before him, as he couldn't possibly have been anyone else but Dianna's husband. Shiye grasped his hand, his face utterly inscrutable.

"Mr. Brittler. Thank you for welcoming me into your home." His voice suggested this kindness was something he hadn't anticipated.

Thomas seemed to hear the words Shiye hadn't spoken. "I'm not ashamed of the choices my daughter has made, son," he said, his blue eyes boring into Shiye's hazel ones.

There came a soft noise of dissent from the door, and Dianna straightened. She knew without having to turn around which member of her family the sound had come from.

Samantha Brittler, Dianna's mother, fixed an icy gaze on Shiye's broad back as she moved into the library. He too, turned at the sound of reproach from her throat. Dianna's father sat up slowly in his wingback armchair and cocked his head to the side politely, eyeing his wife.

"Do you have something to add, Samantha?" he said in his weak voice. She stepped forward, her cold gaze skating over Dianna entirely, as though she had not noticed her eldest daughter was in the room. Samantha was a thin woman. Her back was as straight as a pole and her hair was pulled into an unforgivingly tight knot at the back of her head, not a strand out of place. Her dark brows were raised in a look of outrage, and her shoulders had risen high with indignation as she approached her husband.

"Surely you don't expect us to cater to this savage?" she said, indicating Shiye with a look of disgust. Thomas Brittler's face darkened and he glared at his wife without blinking for several seconds until her face flushed and she had the good grace to look ashamed of her outburst. "But the neighbors will see him, Thomas," she hissed, hardly moving her lips. "They'll see the child."

Dianna felt a sick bile rise in her throat. "The child?" she growled at her mother, stepping forward so that Samantha was forced to look directly into her daughter's eyes. She looked haughty and indifferent. There was no sign of welcome in Samantha Brittler's gaze. No hint of joy at finally seeing the daughter she had been separated from for so many long years. "That child," Dianna spat, taking her mother by the shoulders and turning her so that she was facing Rose. Her daughter cowered behind Shiye's legs, darting terrified glances up at the enigma that was her formidable grandmother. "Is your granddaughter, and my daughter. This *savage*," Dianna stressed the word, the blood pounding in her ears as she indicated her husband. "Is the man I love. I would not be standing here today if it were not for him. I would be dead."

"You would be just fine if you'd only put aside such girlish fantasies of adventure and settled down to a proper marriage, like your sisters." Samantha tilted her head towards Charlotte, Sarah, and Noelle, all of whom flushed, but none so much as Charlotte.

"Are you blind, Mother?!" shouted Dianna. "I married for love. I am happier than I have ever been in my life! Look at Rose. Look at her face. She is your family. Shiye is your family. Have some compassion!"

Her mother swelled, her cheeks flooding with color. "Compassion?" she seethed. Her voice so low it almost blended with the crackling of the fire behind Thomas Brittler's chair. "Where was your compassion, Dianna, when you abandoned your family for something better? Where was your compassion when you dropped us like dirt and ran off to find your own happiness?" Dianna had never seen her mother come apart like this. Samantha Brittler was close to tears, her bosom was heaving in her pinched corset, she looked as though she were about to explode.

"That's enough of this," rasped Thomas Brittler from his chair. He was bent forward, his unsteady gaze darting between his wife and eldest daughter. "Samantha, you know why Dianna left us. She was lonely. She was lost. Not one person in this family knows that feeling better than you, my dear." A tear trickled from the corner of Samantha's eye. "We've all missed her, but she's here now. And look," Thomas held out his hand to tiny little Rose. "Our granddaughter has my nose."

Rose glanced at both her parents before reaching forward to take her grandfather's hand. She gave him the tiniest of smiles, and the whole room let out its collective breath. There was suddenly more air. More sanity.

Dianna turned a slightly softened gaze onto her mother, but Samantha would not meet her eyes. Without looking at anyone, she strolled out of the room, slamming the library door behind her.

"She'll come around," muttered Dianna's father, sitting back in his chair and reaching for a glass of water on the side table. He took a drink and then erupted into a fit of coughing. Little Rose looked up at her father, alarmed by the sick rattle that was coming from the grandfather she had just met. Shiye crouched on the ground next to Thomas's chair.

"There is something I know that may help clear your lungs," he said. "Would you permit me to find the ingredients in your kitchen?"

"Son, if you know something that might help, I'm all ears." Thomas exploded into another coughing fit, his eyes watering. He gestured to Noelle, his voice catching around his next words. "Take Dianna's husband downstairs and help him find what he's after."

Dianna's lower lip quivered as Shiye left the room, casting her an affectionate look as he went. Her other sisters stepped forward and each of them found a seat around their father's chair. Dianna joined them and tilted her head onto her his knee. He gave a soft chuckle and she looked up at him, her eyes full of fear and concern.

"If Noelle were sitting here I'd feel as though I'd of stepped back in time," he said, peering blearily around at them all. "It's been a long while since you've all sat at my feet." He reached across the arm of the chair and lifted a black, leather-bound Bible from its place on the side table.

"Dianna," he said, clearing his throat roughly. "Won't you read to us this evening? I think it would do us good to hear your voice. It's been such a long time."

Dianna nodded and took the Bible from her father's hands. Charlotte and Sarah slid a little closer to listen as Dianna opened it and tried to read through her tears.

They took turns, each of the girls passing the book between them. Eventually, Noelle joined them, saying that Shiye was now stirring a pot full of spices and oddities in the kitchen. She shook her head as she said this. It was clear from her behavior that whatever Shiye had put in the pot was outlandish, but she shrugged as she fluffed out her skirts and sat down to take a turn reading with her sisters.

Rose sat in her mother's lap, staring at the Bible as it was passed from hand to hand. Thomas Brittler stared at her, and when Dianna met his gaze he smiled wearily.

"She looks a lot like you," he said in a whisper over the sound of Noelle's sweet voice.

Dianna smiled. "I think she looks more like Shiye."

"Papa says my eyes are shaped like Mama's, but they have his color," muttered Little Rose unexpectedly. She was watching her grandfather with just as much interest as he was displaying for her.

"Your Papa is quite right, my dear," chuckled Thomas. He gave another small cough and then turned his attention back to his youngest daughter, his eyes flickering to Rose often, as though he could not stop himself from looking at her.

Shiye came in an hour later carrying a cup of some unfortunate green liquid. Dianna raised an eyebrow at him. He merely smiled and handed the cup to his father-in-law. Thomas took it with thanks and wrinkled his nose at the pungent smell that hit him as he went to take a sip.

"Good gracious, son. This smells like a bourbon-basted skunk."

Shiye shrugged apologetically. "It was my grandmother's recipe. Or as close as I could get to it here in New York. I'm afraid she was never much of a cook, but she was a good healer." He smiled fondly. Then grimaced and shrugged again. "I'm afraid it tastes like it smells," he added.

"I don't doubt that," grumbled Thomas. Dianna hovered around him while he pinched his nose and took a swift sip. He swallowed and smacked his lips in a disgusted sort of way, then after a moment, the pained furrow on his brow relaxed. He sighed, closed his eyes, and took another sip.

"That's positively repulsive stuff," he chuckled at Shiye, and Shiye shot him a sheepish grin. "I hope you made a great vat of it."

Shiye nodded with an awkward smile on his lips and watched Thomas take another sip.

Bit by bit, he drained the cup, and as he did so his shoulders became heavy and the tension appeared to leak out of his body. Dianna's father sat back in his chair after a time and reached for the blanket that had fallen to his knees. Dianna bent forward and kissed his cheek and Thomas opened fuzzy eyes to look at her.

"Thank you for coming back to us," he whispered. "I love you, Di."

"I love you too, Father."

"I do believe that I might be able to rest now, though," Thomas said. He patted Dianna's hand and closed his eyes. "Go get settled in for the night. I'm sure you're all exhausted." He looked down at Rose, who peered up at him and smiled toothily.

"I'll see you all in the morning," he whispered. He reached out a hand to tweak Rose's little nose and, one by one, his family tip-toed out of the room to give their father the first restful sleep he'd had in several weeks.

Chapter Seven

Shiye ran his calloused hands through his long, dark hair and gripped it tightly at the scalp, trying to siphon off some of the burning ache throbbing in his temples. It was nightfall. He was standing alone in a room that had evidently been his wife's bedroom when she lived in this massive house with her parents. He'd never seen homes like this before, but he was doing his best to keep his curiosities in check. He'd been quite thrown when he entered the kitchen earlier and found all manner of strange appliances. There was a huge brick and mortar opening that they used for a fireplace. It was incredible. And filled nearly the entire length of the far wall. The walls themselves were decorative and thick, painted in a variety of colors.

This room for example. Shiye approached one of the walls and prodded at the floral patterned paper that covered it. He could see the seams that made him think it had been stuck there on purpose, but he couldn't imagine why anyone would want to put paper covered in flowers all over their walls.

The lights that hung from the ceiling flickered as Shiye examined the wallpaper, and he looked up at the dangling fixtures. There were two of them because the room was so vast. This room was bigger than their entire cabin had been. The cabin he had built with his bare hands for his family to live in. Suddenly, his efforts seemed embarrassingly futile. This grandeur, the strange comforts all around him, Dianna deserved these things. Rose deserved these things. Shiye simply did not belong.

He ceased examining the wallpaper and turned his attentions to the massive canopy bed that dominated the center of the room. As he did so, a shrill giggle sounded from the floor below. Rose was quite enjoying herself.

The poor girl was too much like her father. She could hardly keep her eyes in her head. The buildings of Manhattan that had surrounded the train station were enormous. Shiye and Rose had never seen buildings towering into the skyline like that. He had known of them. Dianna had talked of them, but he still found the idea of people stacking their homes one on top of the other unnerving. In the event of an attack, the white people would be easy targets for their enemies. That was the point, though. Dianna's people had so few enemies, it didn't matter if they stacked their homes on top of each other, or at least that was the impression he got from it.

There were many things that his wife took for granted that were revelations to him. He was confused by all of it, and too embarrassed to ask, for fear of sounding like the ignorant savage they all assumed he was. But he was a savage. He was an Indian. This mess of smoke-belching factories and people squashed together on the streets. It was as different as possible from life in Wyoming. It didn't suit him.

Shiye finished his cursory examination of the bed and sat down on it. The coverlet was made of some fine, silky material. After running his hands over it in fascinated irritation for a few moments, he stood back up and wandered over to the window.

His wife's bedroom was on the second floor of the enormous house. In the garden below, the rain continued to pound the lawn into mud. He could make out many plants he had never seen before, all swaying with the heavy downpour.

There was the sound of footsteps in the hallway and the door handle turned. Dianna entered the room, looking around for Shiye.

She was dazzling. Gone were the smears of dirt and tousled hair from their journey. Gone was the bedraggled brown dress and overcoat she had owned for several years. Her cheeks were pink and the smile on her lips was genuine, although her eyes still looked worried. His wife had donned a simple, elegant, yellow gown and her beautiful, golden hair was wet and dark from the bath she had just taken.

As she stepped into the room, she caught sight of Shiye and then looked around with an air of amusement. "I can't believe they haven't redecorated it," she said with a sad little smirk on her full, pink lips. "It looks exactly the same as it did on the day I left it."

"Do you regret it?" The cruel question tumbled from his mouth before he could stop it.

"Regret what?" asked Dianna, frowning.

Shiye turned and sat down on the bench that lay beneath the window, his arms crossed as he reclined and looked around their sumptuous surroundings, carefully avoiding Dianna's gaze.

"Leaving," he said, trying to hide the sour note in his voice. Dianna was watching him. She hadn't yet moved away from the open doorway, but now she stepped into the room and closed the door behind her.

"Of course I don't regret it," she said. Her hips swayed in their ever-sensual way as she crossed the room toward him, disbelief etched all over her pretty face. Her freckles stood out brilliantly on her cheeks, like stars in a dark sky, but he was still having trouble meeting her steady blue gaze.

"This is," Shiye gestured around the room, searching for the right words. Astounding. Infuriating. "Difficult," he finished finally, not wanting to offend, but still trying to get his point across with a gentle inflection on the word.

Dianna sighed and sat her slender form down on the seat beside them, squishing their bodies together on the cushioned bench.

"Don't," muttered Shiye as she bent her head and snuggled into his shoulder. "You'll get filth all over your dress."

Dianna tilted her head up and looked askance at him. "I don't care an ounce for my dress, Shiye," she exclaimed. "What gives you the idea..." she paused, contemplating him, confused. Then she said: "Ah, I see."

Shiye's shoulders sagged. "You left all this behind," he said. "Your family adores you. Your house is made up of so many different rooms that I got lost on my way back from the kitchen," he scowled. "Why would you ever allow me to keep you from returning to this? Why would you ever leave?"

Dianna giggled and shook her head. "I did not 'allow you to keep me'," she squeaked through her laughter. "It was against my inclination to give you a choice, my darling husband."

Shiye had to laugh too. "Yes, I suppose it was."

He settled quietly beside her for a few moments, tilting his head against hers and stroking his fingers through her damp hair. There came another shrieking giggle from below and he smiled grimly. "Rose seems to be getting along well with her aunties."

"Noelle is positively spoiling her," replied Dianna. She turned her head to glance out the window behind them. "Manhattan always seems dreary in the fall," she said. The colors are pretty, but it's nothing like home, where the trees look like fire on the horizon." Shiye caught the catch in his wife's voice and gave her shoulders a swift squeeze.

"I have to admit, though," he muttered, "I am happy to not be looking over my shoulder every moment. Being so far away has made me realize that perhaps the best way to avoid those hunting us was for us to leave. Now, although I miss it, I wish we had never stayed. We shouldn't have, really. Not so close."

"We were hundreds of miles away from the land your people call home, Shiye. The fact that they found us is something of a chance in itself."

Shiye heaved a sigh as his memories took hold of him, pulling him far away from Dianna's bedroom. He was in a place where the sun shone on fields of battle. He was to be the glorious bringer of peace. Him, with Kuckunniwi's daughter by his side. They were to work together and be one. He shuddered. He saw his wife-to-be shouting at Matchitehew's child. He watched the girl fall. Felt the blood on his hands. So much blood.

Dianna was still talking, and Shiye tugged himself back to the present with difficulty. She was looking at him with concern.

"You should rest," she whispered. "Why don't you take a turn in the bath? The water should be warm now."

"Warm?" chuckled Shiye, and he stood. "Perhaps I prefer the ice of the river."

"Perhaps you should take better care of your fingers and toes," smirked his wife. She stood too, absently brushing away the dust he had left on her skirts. "I'll show you where it is and then bring you some fresh clothes."

"Not my leathers," mumbled Shiye hurriedly, without thinking.

Dianna shook her head from side to side in amusement and stood on her tiptoes to press a kiss to his lips. Shiye kept her at arm's length, still trying to keep her dress from staining.

"I am not a porcelain doll, my dear," she responded irritably.

Her closeness distracted him from his gloomy thoughts. "If you would like to convince me of that," he whispered, an evil glint flickering into his eyes, "you will have to take off that ridiculous dress."

The warm bath was something of a delight, although he would never admit it to his wife. The heat of it relaxed his back muscles and calmed his nerves. He even managed to quit looking around the "bathroom" skeptically as he sunk to his shoulders in the giant tin basin. He was awoken by his own snore a few moments before Dianna knocked on the door and entered, closing it behind her. She was talking as she came into the room and Shiye had to scrub his fists into his eyes before he could focus on what she was saying to him.

"I've just seen Sarah's husband talking to Rose," she said with a grin. "He was always the very pleasant sort. He and Sarah are such a good match. Their children are downstairs as well. Sleeping in the rooms across from the sitting room, I think. They said they wouldn't mind if Rose slept in there with them, and while they do keep staring at her skin, I do think that they will treat her kindly."

"Sarah has children?" Shiye asked groggily, sitting up in the foggy water and shaking his head to rid his ears of liquid.

"You know she does," said Dianna, busily laying out the clothes she had brought in with her. "I can't believe how much time has passed," she said sadly. "I have missed them all so much."

"I'm sorry, Di," said Shiye, reaching out a gentle hand towards her with a sad smile of his own. "At least that will be different," he whispered, pressing a kiss to his wife's fingers as he drew her closer to him.

"What will?" asked Dianna, absentmindedly following the pressure of his hand on hers.

"When I've enough money, we can buy a home close by. That way you can see them more often." Shiye turned himself sideways in the small tub, causing water to lap at the sides.

Dianna looked confused. "You mean to stay here? In Manhattan?" She rolled up her long sleeves and lifted a sponge from the table behind her.

"If it would make you happy," whispered Shiye. Dianna's tender, warm fingers tickled their way over his back as she nudged him forward and began rubbing a bar of soap over his shoulders and spine. She looked thoughtful.

"It would be wonderful to be somewhere closer. To not have to hide..." She trailed the tips of her fingers over the heavy scars that marred his back. Evidence of the punishment inflicted on him by his father when he had returned home from Kuckunniwi's land and confessed his failures.

Her touch was like a balm on his frayed senses. No, he did not like the idea of remaining here, of struggling to find work when not a soul would be able to look past the color of his skin, but he would do it. He'd do it for Dianna and Rose. He would willingly live in a place that he could already tell he would despise. He would do it if it would make his wife happy. If it meant his family would be safe.

"I don't want to live here," she breathed onto the back of his neck, scrubbing the sponge over the front of his chest. "I already miss home."

"There is no home to go back to, Dianna," he said, catching hold of her hand and tilting his face to look up at hers. "Why should we not try to build a life somewhere secure? Protected. Somewhere Matchitehew will never find us, never be near Rose, not ever again."

"Here though?" queried Dianna doubtfully.

Shiye gave her a twisted grin. "Well," he said with a shrug of his massive shoulders, "Perhaps not in the bathroom of your father's home..."

Dianna smacked him playfully with the wet sponge and he ceased his teasing as vile, soapy water splashed into his mouth, making him gag. Dianna pursed her lips, hiding a smile.

Chapter Eight

As her father's health grew worse and then better and then worse again, she began to feel comfortable in her family's home once more. Granted, her mother still wouldn't look her in the eye and she treated both Shiye and Rose like dogs that had rolled in something smelly, but apart from Samantha Brittler's sour disposition there was no reason for Dianna to feel unwelcome.

Noelle, Sarah, and Charlotte, she found out, all lived within a few hours ride of the Brittler House with their husbands. When Thomas had fallen ill, they had promptly made themselves at home once more, unable to stand being separated by such a great distance when his health was so precarious.

"Tell us of the Indians again, Di," pleaded Noelle. All four sisters were sitting in the Library with their father, needlework in hand, and chatting amicably about the events of the past few years in hushed tones while Thomas snored gently in the corner. He had fallen asleep during Sarah's unfortunately dull tale of what it was like to be married to the perfect man with the perfect children and the perfect house in the country. Dianna loved Sarah dearly, but her contented happiness lacked the thrill of the illicit, and Noelle and Charlotte continuously turned to Dianna in attempts to liven up the conversation.

"Or about that Parker Jameson," whispered Noelle, "He seems like an interesting character."

Dianna shook her head at her sisters. "There's nothing more to tell," she said.

"Shiye and I built our little house next to a river, hundreds of miles away from his people. We didn't think they'd follow us over the mountains, but... Matchitehew found us."

"And was he truly playing with Rose the entire time? How could you not know?"

Dianna felt a painful twinge of guilt at Charlotte's question. Her fiery-haired sister had always been the bluntest of the foursome.

Dianna sighed. "I don't know, Lottie, I honestly don't know how we could have missed it. Shiye is an excellent tracker. He can hunt a squirrel through a briar patch and come out the other side without a scratch on him. He was constantly on the watch. There was never any sign that anyone had been on the property. I just don't understand...." she wiped a traitorous tear on her needlework and looked up at her sisters. "We're safe here, that's all that matters."

Three children entered the room at that moment and scampered like quiet little mice to tug on their mothers' skirts.

"It's stopped raining outside, Mama," whispered Rose, giving Dianna a wide look of longing. "Thomas and Mary want to go and play outside in the garden. Can't I go too?"

Dianna looked across the room where Thomas, Sarah's oldest son, named for his grandfather, and Mary, his younger sister, were fidgeting excitedly, hoping for permission. She looked up questioningly at her sister, who shrugged.

"You may play in the garden," she said to Rose, who was practically vibrating with excitement, "but wear your warm boots and change into your brown dress."

"Yes, Mama," Rose said with a nod and she stood on her toes to give her mother a kiss on the cheek. Her long, dark hair was braided into a plait down her back and the almost invisible freckles on her round cheeks were standing out in her flushed face.

As the three moved quietly out of the room, cautious of their sleeping grandfather, Dianna stood and stretched.

"I think I'll go watch the children playing in the yard. I can't seem to let Rose very far out of my sight recently, not since..." she sighed, and moved toward the door.

"Di," said her father's voice from the depths his chair.

"Yes, Father?" she moved immediately over to his side, taking hold of his outstretched hand.

He was looking refreshed after his long sleep and his grip on her hands felt stronger than it had for several days now. She took this as a good sign.

"You are safe here," he muttered so that only she could hear him. "You need not fear that man while you stay in my home." Dianna gave her father's hand a squeeze.

"I know," she said.

She found Rose in the garden a few minutes later, talking circles around her laughing father. Shiye looked up as Dianna approached.

"I don't really want her out in the yard alone," he whispered into her ear, and Dianna nodded.

"Nor I," she said. "I was just on my way out."

Shiye's mouth was a thin line of worry as his eyes skated over the exposed foliage around the property. "How is your father today?" he inquired, his voice still low as he watched Rose flounce across the lawn to join her cousins.

"A little stronger, I think."

"Good. I thought he looked better yesterday as well."

"What's that you have there?" asked Dianna. She had just noticed Shiye was holding the day's paper.

"Oh, I-uh-" he was suddenly looking sheepish as he tried to hide the paper behind his back. Dianna raised her eyebrows at him. "Oh, alright," he said, as though he was admitting to some dreadful crime. "Sarah's husband has been teaching me to read English."

"Really?" exclaimed Dianna, breaking into a broad grin. "That is very nice of him. I recall trying to do something similar a little while after we were married and..."

"Don't start," said Shiye, holding up his hand to fend her off. "I know I've limited patience for the subject, but I am *trying*." He said this last word looking quite irascible. "I was searching the paper for possible positions."

Dianna's face fell. "You're still determined then?"

"Only because I believe it will make you happy and make us safe," he whispered. Shiye put his arm around Dianna's waist and they both turned at a shout from the trees. It was Thomas, he was pushing his sister and Rose on the rope swing and all three of them were laughing uproariously.

"They do get along well, don't they?" remarked Dianna, watching the way Rose's face was shining with delight. Their daughter had never had friends her own age to play with before.

"They have the same blood running through their veins," said Shiye proudly.

There were some moments when Shiye's warrior heritage looked out from behind his eyes. In being together for six years, the two had developed an unspoken agreement to honor the traditions of both of their families; to speak both languages and live both lives. It felt natural and easy. So much so that Dianna often forgot that, before her, Shiye had been a fierce warrior. A man of honor and tradition. He was still this, but occasionally it manifested itself more distinctly.

Dianna loved the pride with which he was watching his daughter dance and play, she loved the fiery, insurmountable force that emanated from him. This man, this *warrior*, he didn't belong in Manhattan. He would never be happy here.

"I don't want to stay here, Shiye," she whispered again.

His shoulders heaved in a sigh and he looked down at her. He looked worn, one hundred years old.

"I'm so tired of running, Di," he said. He took hold of her hand. "Let's put that all behind us. We could build a life here."

Dianna sighed again and looked over at Rose. She memorized the beautiful smile on her daughter's face. "I will follow you," she said simply to Shiye.

He brought the back of her hand to his lips and kissed it with a tenderness that defied words.

....

There they were. Matchitehew settled himself into the cover of the trees, watching the tiny family with hate and repulsion. It hadn't been easy getting here. But it would be worth it, all worth it, when he could finally exact his revenge. The coward before him had taken away everything he'd ever loved. There was no room for compassion, no room for pity. This `*Shiye*' was the reason his daughter no longer drew breath in this world. He had murdered her in cold blood. A child just like his own, `Little Rose'. The day was approaching.

His Bena had been five years old when she had been torn from him. Matchitehew thought himself justified for waiting five years after their daughter was born to take her. He wanted them to know it was he who punished them for their happiness. For daring to love when his love was no more.

They were complacent, thinking he would never follow them here. But Matchitehew was patient. He had built a relationship with their tiny one. It would make it that much easier to convince her to come with him when it was time.

He imagined the horrified look on the white woman's face when she had seen him on the train station platform. Delicious.

......

Dianna brought the children inside as evening began to fall around them. On their way into the house, they passed her mother going out.

"Where are you going at such a late hour?" Dianna called. Samantha cast a severe look over her eldest daughter. She ignored Shiye and Rose completely as she stepped out the front door.

"To town," she stated.

"Alone?" Dianna had halted in the doorway.

"Yes, alone, Dianna," Samantha snapped as she climbed into the cart waiting there.

"You can't go alone," grouched Dianna, stubbornly. She reached for her coat. "I'll go with you."

With that, she swung her coat over her shoulders, kissed her daughter and her husband, and marched out after her mother.

It was a very uncomfortable ride into town. Dianna did not try to force her mother into conversation. She had tried that several times already with no success. They both sat in silence looking out of opposite windows as the footman cracked the reins.

"There was no need for you to accompany me, Dianna. I am perfectly capable of doing my errands alone."

"What sensible woman goes out after dark by herself in Manhattan?" Dianna growled at her mother, adjusting her coat around her shoulders and tugging her long hair out her collar. "Father wouldn't have dreamed of letting you come alone."

"Your father doesn't need to know," fumed Samantha, crossing her arms in front of her chest in a characteristically irksome posture. Dianna tried to hold in her temper. She had come to make things better with her mother, after all, not to worsen them. It felt like Samantha was putting up a wall with the gesture. Keeping herself from Dianna as she so often had in her childhood.

Samantha Brittler had never been an affectionate mother. She wasn't the type to read stories or sing songs often. She was the sort of person who thought that improper behavior ought to be punishable by law. It wasn't necessarily her fault either. She'd had the idea drilled into her. First by her own mother, then by her private school, then by her first husband. It wasn't so much of a shock that she should protest entirely to Thomas Brittler's liberal way of running his household. What was a shock was that she hadn't grown accustomed to it in their nearly thirty years of marriage.

"Where are we going, Mother?" begged Dianna after they had passed into the heart of the city.

Samantha Brittler was silent. Dianna bent forward and poked the woman, her patience stretched to the breaking point. "Where are we going?" she repeated.

Samantha sighed with irritation.

"We're going to the herbalist," she stated with a bluntness that reminded Dianna forcibly of Charlotte.

"Why?"

Her mother chewed her tongue, as though Dianna's voice was grating on her last nerve, then she snapped: "I overheard your husband speaking about an herb we didn't have in the kitchen. I special ordered it and a few others for his drink he has been making for your father. I'm astounded to say that I think the disgusting concoction might actually be aiding his recovery." She said all of this very fast, as though it would be less unpleasant for her to get it over with quickly.

Dianna raised an eyebrow. "You mean to tell me," she couldn't keep amusement from creeping into her voice, "that my savage husband is actually an intelligent human?" She put a hand on her chest in mock-surprise. "Goodness, I never would have guessed!" Her voice dripped sarcasm.

"Don't be lewd with me, child. It's very unbecoming."

Dianna had to roll her eyes.

Her mother glared at her. "I don't know what to make of your behavior, Dianna, I really don't."

"Mother," snapped Dianna. "I'm tired of this act you're putting on. I'm sick of you avoiding me and my family like the plague." She reached forward and grasped her mother's shoulders. "I'm sorry I left you. I'm sorry you feel as though I abandoned you. I'm sorry that I wasn't content to marry into society and be the perfect little gem of a daughter you always wanted. I wanted to be happy. Is that such a terrible thing?"

Samantha observed her daughter coolly for a moment. The ever-present mask of propriety slipping a little. Her expression was stony, but her blue eyes were filled with tears.

"You left us behind to search for your happiness," she choked. "Was your family not enough?"

"I never intended it to be so long," whispered Dianna. Guilt was exploding like firecrackers in her insides. "I was foolish to go. I know I was. But I do *not* regret it."

The tears in her mother's eyes began flooding down her slender cheeks. She raised a gloved hand to Dianna's face. "My little girl," she said. "You broke my heart when you left me."

"I didn't mean too, Mother. Truly, I didn't."

They were both crying now. For the first time in what felt like forever, Samantha Brittler folded her daughter into her arms. They sobbed all the way to the shop, and only stopped when the footman hammered on the roof of the carriage.

"I'll just be a moment!" her mother called, and she slid away from Dianna, straightening her hat and wiping at her eyes. "Well, then," she huffed, bestowing a thin-lipped smile on her daughter. "What do you say we wander into this smelly little shop and pick up our parcels?"

Dianna nodded numbly, still reeling from her glimpse behind her mother's mask.

When they next sat back down in the carriage, Dianna's mother was her usual stoic self once more. "I mean, really. What good could all these little leaves and berries do for your father?" she asked flippantly. But Dianna now understood why her mother had chosen to journey to the herbalists alone at night. Heaven forbid anyone might see her catering to Shiye's wishes. Heaven forbid anyone in the family see how much she cared.

Samantha Brittler was sick with worry, with fear. She had lost one husband before. She had no desire to lose the man she loved this time around. She would do everything and anything she could to see that he was made well again, even if that meant taking advice from a man whom she heartily disliked and mistrusted.

Another tap on the roof announced their arrival and Dianna exited the carriage after her mother, smiling grimly. Yes, her mother was a particular brand of odd with her proclivities towards the proper and perfect. She knew this. She had always known this.

Deep on the inside, where her mother felt it safe to hide her feelings, she held a passionate heart. One that loved fiercely and with no reservations. Unfortunately, her mother's heart surrounded itself with a wall of thorns, because it was terrified of breaking.

Chapter Nine

Her father's uphill climb continued, and the healthier he became, the more Dianna relaxed. His pasty white skin thickened somehow and began to regain some of its usual pallor. He began to put on weight, and laugh with something of his usual gusto.

Dianna cornered Shiye one afternoon in the hallway outside the library as he was bringing her father another cup.

"Thank you," she whispered. This was not the first time she had said this. She had been thanking Shiye every day for his efforts. However, today was different. Her father had gained his feet easily several times this morning, and breathed without effort. The deathly rattle had vanished from his lungs.

"You're most welcome," Shiye whispered back, he placed a smart kiss on the tip of Dianna's nose and smiling, walked into the library.

"My daily dose!" Dianna heard her father sing from the other side of the door. She beamed as she moved away down the hallway.

Rose had been nervously avoiding her grandmother since their first furious introduction.

"Grandma is mean," she would mumble to Dianna, anytime she was forced to remain in her presence for long enough for her grandmother to give her a contemptuous look. "Why is she so mean, Mama?"

"I really don't know, darling."

If Dianna had hoped that her mother would have softened towards her daughter after their conversation in the carriage, she had hoped in vain. Dianna glowered at Samantha each time Rose shrank back in fear against her leg.

"What is it that you can't stand mother? That she is an Indian? Or that she is evidence of your disagreement with my decisions? Do you so desire to have me under your thumb that you cannot show kindness to my child?"

At this, her mother's nostrils had flared and she had turned from Dianna with a swish of her skirts and stormed from the room.

Shiye was, as yet, untroubled by Samantha's ire. "If one woman should despise me, only one, from your large family, then I am luckier, by far, then I ever imagined I would be by coming here. I only wish she would treat Rose more kindly. I think her grandmother's behavior is starting to have an effect on her."

Although Rose was enjoying her cousins, her aunties and her uncles, all of whom were unfailingly kind towards her, she continued to ask the same question. "When will we go home, Mama. When can we go back?"

Dianna had not yet had the heart to tell their daughter that they would not be returning to their peaceful cabin by the river. She knew that to delay was only going to do more harm than good, but she couldn't bring herself to watch Rose's face fall, as she knew it would; she didn't want to be the one who brought agonizing tears to her eyes. So she delayed.

....

The days were creeping by and he lived, cloaked in shadow, his furious hunger as nothing to his hate.

He watched. He waited for the opportune moment. It was nearly time.

....

Shiye stood beside the fire stirring for a few minutes, humming softly to himself and trying to avoid breathing in the putrid fumes issuing from the depths of large pot before him. Dianna's father's health was improving and for that, he was thankful. He hated to think that he was causing a rift between Dianna and her mother, and he felt that the sooner they got out from under her feet, the happier she would be.

Thomas Brittler had been more welcoming than Shiye had ever thought possible. *Son,* he called him. *Son.* Shiye had never thought there would be a man he respected as much as he respected Thomas Brittler. To put aside the fact that his daughter had married a man so very different from himself, a true *savage* in his mind. It was an act of courage that Shiye himself could marvel at.

He turned to look at Rose, who sat behind him on a wooden stool. She was butted up to the tall counter and her short legs were swinging energetically as she colored on a spare bit of parchment. Shiye imagined her leaving him, running across the country to live far away. Marrying a man that he had never met, nor given his blessing to, and his blood boiled at the thought. Which made his respect for Thomas rise still farther, although he felt rather incredulous. How had the man done it?

There was a clatter from the doorway and Noelle entered the room, her arms full fresh flowers and her expression full of meaning.

"Shiye," she said, coming right up to him. "Father wishes to speak with you."

Shiye raised his eyebrows at her. "About the drink? It's nearly ready. I'll bring him up a cup in a moment."

Noelle shook her head. She looked very much like Dianna. Her nose was freckly and her eyes were kind, but Dianna was lean and willowy, where Noelle was full-figured. "He's come down from the library," she whispered. "He's dressed and everything. He's sat down on the front porch."

Shiye smiled. "That's wonderful news. I'll go to him. Do you mind keeping an eye on the pot?"

Noelle stepped into the scullery room off the kitchen and sat down her burden, returning after only a moment and tying an apron around her waist. She took the wooden spoon with which he had been stirring and wrinkled her nose at the smell.

Grinning, Shiye went to leave the room, hesitating for only a moment to pat his daughter on the back and peer over her shoulder at her drawing. "That is very nice, darling," he said.

"It's Chew," whispered Rose sadly, holding it up for her father to see. "I miss him terrible."

Shiye felt his blood run cold and he had to work not to snatch the picture from his daughter's hands and toss it into the fire. "Rose-" he began.

"I know you said he was a bad man, Papa, but he was always so very nice to me."

"He was pretending," said Shiye harshly. "He *is* a *bad* man, Rose, whatever else he might have made you think of him. He wants to kill us all."

"Then you should ask him not to," whispered Rose. "I'm sure he will agree that killing is a dreadful thing. We talked about it once." She scratched her nose absently and tilted her head up to gaze into Shiye's face. Her round, innocent eyes refused to understand.

"He lost his daughter like me, a long time ago, before I was born. Someone killed her."

Tiponi's mad face flashed before Shiye's eyes. He swallowed roughly. "Yes," he murmured, "someone did kill her."

"Who?"

"A terrible woman," Shiye said, "a woman with no kindness in her heart."

"A woman like Grandmother?" Rose lowered her voice conspiratorially as Noelle snorted with amusement behind them. Shiye glanced at her and shook his head.

"No, not like Grandmother. Your grandmother is kind in her heart, even if she doesn't know how to show it properly."

There was the sound of a throat clearing in the doorway and Samantha Brittler entered the room. The look on her face told Shiye that she had overheard the conversation between him and his daughter. He met her eyes unflinchingly and gave her a nod. He was quite astounded to see a small smile slide onto her lips.

She sighed, walked across the kitchen, and retrieved a jar from one of the top shelves. Rose had leapt from her seat and scuttled around behind Shiye, her expression wary.

"Thomas and Mary have asked for a cookie," she said, setting the jar down on the table without looking at any of them. She laid out three saucers and, one by one, removed a cookie from the jar and placed it on each. Without saying a word, she lifted the third saucer with a cookie on it and sat it down over the top of Rose's drawing, then turned and left the room.

Rose clambered back up onto her stool at once and bit into the cookie with enthusiasm.

"You see?" said Shiye, giving his daughter's long braid a playful tug, "She just doesn't know how to show it."

Rose shrugged.

"Be sure to tell her thank you for the cookie the next time you see her," he said to her. Rose cast him a dubious look and went back to her treat.

Feeling as though they had taken a minuscule step forward with his mother-in-law, Shiye left the room in search of Dianna's father.

It didn't take him long to find him. Thomas Brittler was wearing a broad grin on his face as he sat on one of the two wicker chairs on the front porch. He gestured to the second chair as Shiye came out to greet him.

"In all honesty," Thomas said, looking out at the damp front garden as it was flooded with autumn sunlight. "I never thought I'd leave that room."

"You had us all very worried," Shiye responded as he sat down stiffly in the wicker chair. Never having had a one on one conversation with his father-in-law, he felt distinctly uncomfortable.

"Might not have come out of it if it hadn't been for you," muttered Thomas.

He was looking right at Shiye, and he met his gaze with a swift nod. "I'm glad I could help."

"Perhaps it was a good thing," Thomas noted. He returned his eyes to the yard. "If I hadn't been so very unwell, I may never have met my daughter's husband and child. I may never have seen my daughter again."

"She wouldn't have stood for that," stated Shiye firmly. "She talked of you every day. Missed each and every one of you. Sometimes, though she tried to hide it, I would hear her crying in the night."

"She loves you," said Thomas, his cheeks rather pink. He tapped his fist on his knee. "Never seen her look at anything the way she looks at you and that girl."

"I know," muttered Shiye with a smile. "I was blessed the day she came into my life." He paused and then went rambling on. "Stubborn as a mule, your daughter," he said with a small chuckle. "I tried to send her home. I tried to make her leave... She wouldn't go."

"Yes," laughed Thomas. "Once she sets her mind on something, it's impossible to change it. She's been that way since she was small."

Shiye shook his head. "I owe you several apologies," he said to Thomas and the man looked at him in confusion. "What for?"

"I never meant to bring her into harm's way."

Thomas sat for a moment, as though he was digesting Shiye's words. "I don't believe you did, son," he said finally. "But, she wanted an adventure. Well, here you are. Her adventure. Her savior as well, from what I hear. You saved her from that wretched man she went to marry."

Shiye said nothing. He didn't know how to respond.

"Perhaps things have turned out the way they were meant to," Thomas acknowledged, watching a bird flutter down onto the porch railing.

Shiye was reminded suddenly of the medicine man's son who had saved him from being murdered by Tiponi's people. He saw, in his mind's eye, the knowing face of the older man in the distance. He saw Dianna's golden hair as she walked beneath the tree he had chosen to spend the night in. What had made her walk under *that* tree? Shiye saw every little detail that had brought him to this place, this moment. Sitting beside the father of a wife he never, in his wildest dreams, thought he would call his own. His eyes grew unaccountably misty. Surely, some divine intervention had occurred to bring him to this place.

Shiye swallowed, his eyes on the bird as well. "I wanted to apologize too, for never having managed to ask for your blessing, sir. If I could have, I would have."

"You have it," responded Thomas, and he looked back at Shiye. "It doesn't take much for a father to know a good man from a lousy one." He shook his head morosely. "I told Charlotte... Well, that is neither here, nor there. The point is, I believe you're a good man, Shiye, and I don't care one wink about the color of your skin or the way you were brought up. I'd rather know my daughter married a good man than some well-to-do gentleman of the first water who wouldn't pay her any mind."

Shiye nodded his thanks. "I can't explain how much I appreciate your kindness."

"Look after my daughter and my granddaughter and you'll always have it."

"I would give my life for them, sir."

Thomas let loose a great sigh, a look of peaceful content sliding onto his face. "So would I, son, so would I."

Chapter Ten

.....

The girl was playing in the garden and she was alone. He'd circled the vast dwelling twice, peering carefully into each of the windows. One of the women was in the kitchen, stirring a pot. Four of them were playing some sort of card game in the sitting room. There were two children sitting on the floor by their feet. Two of the men had left the house early. They did this often, never returning until the evening. The man who murdered his child sat on the front porch with the fourth man of the house.

There were three servants. One who maintained the garden, he only came twice a week. A young woman who lived in the house, at the moment darning clothes in an upstairs window seat. He could see her looking out on the front lawn. The third was a man who managed the barn and brought the carriage around whenever any of the occupants of the house wanted to travel into the nearby town.

With so many people in the house, it was incredible that the girl had been left unsupervised. Yet, here she was, twirling madly in the back garden, away from prying eyes. Now was his chance.

Matchitehew cupped his fingers around his mouth and whistled softly. The resonation that emanated from his lips sounded like the call of some gigantic bird. The girl halted her play and looked towards the noise, hesitant. He called to her again, and she took a step towards the sound.

It was their signal. It had always been their signal. Since she was very small. He had groomed the child not to fear him, and somehow her parents had never noticed. It was a miracle. In all their scouting and care, they had always watched for someone to come from a distance to find them, never knowing they had long-since been found.

The girl's eyes were combing the trees. She gave a low whistle, and he responded with another call. She glanced behind her at the big house, and then smiling mischievously, she ran for the trees, straight into his waiting arms.

"I've missed you, Chew!" she whispered into the cloth of his stomach. "I started to think I would never see you again."

"Here, I am," he said to her looking down into her beaming, round face. It was difficult. She reminded so much of his little one, so much of his Bena. Watching her grow had been a kind of satisfying torture to him. Knowing that he would end her life on the same day Bena's life had been stolen from her, it was a sickening thought that made her company almost unbearable.

"Rose," he said with a smile that didn't quite meet his dark eyes, "would you like to go home?"

Rose darted a quick glance behind her to be sure that no one was searching for her. "Papa says you are not to be trusted," she said in a hushed undertone. "He says that you will try to kill me."

"What a horrible thing for him to say," purred Matchitehew, crouching down so that he was on an eye level with the girl. "Do you think I would try to hurt you, Rose?"

"Certainly not!" cried Rose loudly. He flinched at her loud voice, glancing over her shoulder for signs of approach.

"Rose, if you want to go home, you have to come with me now."

"Right now?" she asked, her eyes widening.

"This very moment," he whispered.

"What about Mama and Papa?"

A bird twittered overhead. Matchitehew looked over her small shoulder once more. "Your Mama and Papa want to stay here forever," he said.

"Well, I certainly don't," sighed Rose. "My grandmother is mean. I like my cousins and my aunties and uncles, though," she said brightening. "And grandmother gave me a cookie today."

"Did she now?"

"Yes, she sort of spoke to Papa as well."

Matchitehew heard the sound of the front door opening and shutting and he had to fight the urge to fling the child over his shoulder and run. He couldn't do that. She would make far too much noise.

Rose looked back over her shoulder.

"You want to go home, don't you?" he whispered cajolingly. "Don't you want to go back to Wyoming? If we go quickly, your Mama and Papa will see you are gone and follow us."

"Really?!" squeaked Rose. She shuffled her tiny feet. "I think they will be angry when they find us."

"They might be a little bit, but at least you will all be home."

"Well..." Rose cast a final look toward the house and then held out her pudgy hand to him. "Alright, then. We had better go quick."

....

Dianna stood up from her place at the card table, looking around the room as Shiye entered.

"Where is Rose?" was her first question.

"She's in the kitchen with Noelle," said Shiye consolingly. He smiled at the four women sitting around the table. Samantha Brittler avoided his gaze.

Dianna brushed her hand over her husband's collar as she passed him. His long hair was flowing down his back in straight waves. They hadn't had an entire room to themselves since Rose was born. Having her sleep with her cousins had made Dianna wary at first, but now she was seeing it as something of a delight.

Her and Shiye had found many ways to divert their attention throughout the course of the long night before, and she was feeling distinctly worn from lack of sleep.

"I think I'll look in on her and then have a short nap before dinner," she said. Shiye eyed her interestedly.

"Perhaps I'll join you in that endeavor," he said this very sweetly, so that only Dianna would notice the wicked gleam in his eye.

She nodded to show that his attendance would not be unwelcome and then went in search of her daughter.

Shiye followed her into the hallway, which was empty. As they rounded the corner, Dianna became aware that her husband was practically breathing down her neck.

"Shiye," she chastised, drawing to a halt and spinning so that she was facing him. "I cannot walk with you treading on the hem of my dress."

"If you walk too fast, you will escape me," he muttered suggestively. His arms snaked around her waist as he spoke and his warm breath tickled her cheek.

"Oh, quit it, you," she gasped as his hands encircled her possessively.

"But I don't really want to... and... I don't really have to," growled Shiye. He tugged her body to his with artful force, causing the breath to leap out of her lungs. Dianna felt the heat of his lips as they descended on hers with powerful assertion. He kissed her like she was his prey, his meal. Like he would starve without the taste of her. Dianna felt him shove her into the wall with abandon, and she gave a tiny squeak of surprise.

He deepened their kiss, and they stood entwined for several long moments before Shiye relinquished his grip on her. Dianna felt a distinct sense of loss envelop her stomach.

He gave her earlobe a nibble and then moved away from her, straightening his vest.

"I just want to look in on Rose," she said breathlessly. Shiye nodded.

"I'll meet you upstairs."

Noelle was sitting at the kitchen table when Dianna entered, reading a magazine. The pungent smell of her husband's health drink filled the space and made her wretch slightly. Noelle glanced up at her. "You get used to it after a little while," she laughed. Dianna held the sleeve of her purple dress over her nose and crossed the kitchen to open the only window.

Waving away the smell and trying not to choke on it, Dianna looked around the room for her daughter. "Where's Rose?"

"She went out into the garden to play," Noelle said unconcernedly.

"Oh," said Dianna, trying not to betray the flicker of fear that danced into her stomach. "How long has she been out there?"

"Only a half an hour or so," said Noelle, catching sight of her sister's face. "Is there something wrong, Di?"

A sick feeling was spiraling up from a deep well in her chest and making its way into her throat. A feeling of foreboding that she had to fight with every step she took towards the back door. She gave Noelle a straight-lipped smile as she spun the handle and stepped out into the yard.

"Rose?" she called, peering around at the trees. The yard was fenced in short, white planks and surrounded by a tall growth of trees which afforded them much privacy from the nearby street and anyone who came to call. "Rose? Where are you?"

For no reason, Dianna's heart began to race. *Calm down,* she told herself. *There's no reason to get upset. She would be perfectly safe in the back garden.* She couldn't seem to stop herself. As the moments crept by with no response from her daughter, Dianna began stalking around the side of the house, peering under bushes, turning on the spot. "Rose!?" she yelled again and again with the sick feeling blossoming inside her like yeast dough overflowing its pan. "Rose?!"

Once she had ascertained that her daughter was not hiding in the yard, she darted back into the house.

"What's the matter," cried Noelle, looking alarmed at the expression on her sister's face.

"She's not in the yard," exclaimed Dianna, staring wildly around the kitchen.

"She's here somewhere, Di, don't fret," said Noelle, climbing to her feet at once. Together, they left the white-tiled kitchen and made their way through the lower levels of the house. When they reached the sitting room, the rest of the family joined in the search.

"What's all the fuss?" asked her father, popping his head through the front door and looking around as his family dashed hither and thither, peeking behind all of the curtains and calling Rose's name.

Shiye descended the stairs that led to the upper floor.

"Is Rose with you?" cried Dianna as she flashed passed him.

"No," he said rotating on his heel and hurrying after his wife. They went room to room, calling for their daughter. Dianna was half-crying.

"Where is she, Shiye? Where could she have gone?"

"I don't know," he growled. "But we'll find her. She's here, probably just fallen asleep in the sitting room or something."

But an hour later there was still no sign of Little Rose. The family had expanded into the yard and the street beyond. The footman and Shiye had gone to the neighbors' houses.

"He has her. Matchitehew. He has her." Dianna knew it in the depths of her soul. Matchitehew had found them. He had taken their little girl, and now they had to go. She grabbed her coat from the hook by the door and launched herself into the night without a second thought. She was at the train station in a matter of moments but cried out with fury upon discovering that the last train heading west had departed an hour ago.

"That's what he did," she said to herself, tugging at her hair. "He took her, and then he boarded the train. He's gone."

"Ma'am?" A small boy of around eleven years old and missing one of his front teeth was tugging on her coat. "Are you Dianna?"

Dianna halted, staring down at the child and hardly seeing him. "Ma'am? Are you Miss Dianna Weston, married to an Indian man called Shiye Weston?"

"I-I am she, yes," Dianna gulped.

"I have a message for you from a man called Chew." Dianna's heart leapt into her throat. "He says you'll need a fast horse."

Chapter Eleven

They switched horses in every town, galloping across the distance. Her body ached and they were still miles behind the train.

"Where would he take her?" she asked Shiye, but he had no answer for her. They had left Manhattan in a blur of confusion and terror. Her family had shouted warnings, called for the constable and at last, promised they would be right behind her. It didn't matter. It was all meaningless noise to Dianna. She kissed her father's cheek and told him they would see each other again soon and then she had fled into the darkness on the back of the fastest horse she could find. They rode alongside the tracks, keeping a wary ear out for the sounds of an approaching train car. Knowing they would have to leap aboard if they were given the chance.

Dianna alternated between terror and fury. If she ever got ahold of the woman that had destroyed their lives, she would rip Tiponi limb from limb.

It all came back to her. All of it. Her lies had condemned Shiye, and now they condemned her daughter. Matchitehew would never believe Shiye hadn't murdered his child. In his mind, his vengeance was justified. Dianna, strangely, understood Matchitehew. She felt his fury, his agony and his need for revenge because she knew she would hunt him to the ends of the Earth if he hurt her daughter. She wouldn't ever give up. It had been another foolish thing to think he would never follow them here. Of course he'd followed them, tracked them, found them. Of course he had.

Dianna suddenly saw Matchitehew's plan as clearly as though he was whispering it in her ear.

He wanted to make Shiye feel as he felt. He wanted to rob him of everything he had ever loved and suck the very life from his veins. He wanted him to watch, and that's why he had told them to come. He was going to kill Rose. He was going to murder her in front of her father's eyes.

Dianna urged the exhausted horse beneath her even faster. There was a town ahead. They would switch horses and ride through the night. They wouldn't stop. They would get there in time.

She told herself this over and over as her body begged her to give up, as her head pounded and her bones throbbed with every step that the horse took. *They would get there in time.*

They caught a train heading West that had come from the South and finally, they rested. Shiye's knuckles were bloody and cracked from the grip he had maintained on each of his horses' reins. Dianna's hips were bruised from the break-neck journey from Manhattan. *Rose. Rose. Rose.* Her daughter's name reverberated in her head. *Lord, keep her safe for me. Forgive me for my negligence. Forgive me for my many sins. Please, Lord. Keep her safe. Let us reach her. Give us the words and the ideas we will need to get her back from this monster.*

Shiye had hardly spoken since they had started their journey West. There hadn't been much room for talking while they road horse-back for fear they might bite off their tongues. Now, though, Dianna felt his silence like the pounding of a judge's gavel on her heart.

"I'm sorry," she whispered. She reached for his hand. Shiye looked at her, and he looked like a man that had lived a thousand days of misery since she had last looked into his eyes.

"What is it that you have to be sorry for?" he hissed, his red-rimmed eyes blazing suddenly fire-bright. "What is it that you have done to bring this horror down on our family? Nothing. The blame lies with me, and with me alone. Dianna, I will save our daughter, I will bring her home to you, and then I will destroy every person that would ever hunt us. I will not run. I will not let them take anything from you ever again. You will never have to run, or hide, or fear from the moment your daughter is back in your arms. I will make sure of that." He turned away from her as she reached out for him.

"This is not your fault," she whispered, and she felt she would sob if there had been any tears left in her body.

"Whose fault is it then?" demanded Shiye. He turned his tortured face to Dianna, and she could see he was as mad with grief as was she.

"You know who has done this to our family, and it wasn't you."

Shiye's body relaxed. "I will find Tiponi," he murmured, I will destroy her for what she has done to us.

Although Dianna agreed with her husband, she was terrified by the expression of his face. She had never imagined Shiye's gentle, loving countenance could display such hate. Such violence. "You cannot undo what has happened, Shiye, and you cannot seek vengeance. It will destroy your soul with its heat."

Shiye didn't seem to hear her. She pressed her cold fingers into his and rested her head against the seat back. The train moved too slow. They still had so much farther to go.

They arrived in Cheyenne at seven in the morning on a Wednesday. It took them another two days to reach Hunton's Ranch. They were watching for signs of Matchitehew all the while, and Dianna was itching for action, for something, anything. She couldn't close her eyes. She kept having the same dream. A nightmare of fire. Of screams. Of searching for something she had lost, something that would never answer her, no matter how she cried.

They stopped to pick up Tanulonli and Tawny from the blacksmith and paid him for his trouble with what little money they had left.

"Twas a fella like you here a few hours ago," said the blacksmith, wiping off their saddles with a filthy rag and indicating Shiye's dark skin. "Said to tell ya," the blacksmith frowned while Dianna held her breath, trying not to shake the words out of the man. "'Ee said ta tell ya he'd be lookin' for ya. Said he'd see ya where the river runs red."

Dianna mouthed silently at Shiye.

"Where the river runs red?" reiterated Shiye, staring hard at the blacksmith as though trying to detect a lie in the man's eyes.

"Yep, that be what he said. Strange fella. Creepy fella. Had a little girl with him."

Dianna and Shiye exchange looks and flung themselves onto their horse's backs. Tawny snorted in welcome, and at last, Dianna felt she would find her home. She would find her daughter. Amidst the terror, amidst her desperate need for haste and vengeance, she felt hope.

It was bitterly cold in the mountains. The snow was thick on the top of Laramie Peak, they couldn't make it over, even though over was the shortest route. They skirted around the mountain and took a zig-zagging path over the rocky ledges.

"He meant the river on Tiponi's land. The place where his daughter died. He's taking Rose there," jumbled Shiye, his teeth chattering with the cold.

"We have to rest, Shiye, or we'll never make it," Dianna sobbed. Her fingers were frozen on the reins, her heart heavy once more.

Shiye looked back over his shoulder and his furious gaze softened. "We should rest," he whispered over the rush of the cool wind. "I have a feeling we'll be needing to fight, and I can't do so with my bones frozen and weary."

Dianna nodded, her cheeks stinging with cold, and they led their horses into the shelter of the nearby clump of trees.

They recovered for as long as they dared. The sun set around them, and they huddled together by a small fire for warmth. Dianna urged her eyes to close, chanted her body to sleep, to no avail. Each time she shut her eyes she saw the evil, grinning face of the Indian man on the train station platform as he waved goodbye to Rose on their final day in Cheyenne. She saw Little Rose holding his hand, playing with him. She saw him slit her daughter's throat over and over again. She couldn't breathe. Terror gripped her. *We will get there in time.*

Dianna clung to her husband. He was rigid with tension. He stroked her hair with a hand that felt as hard and flat as a blade. They moved on before the dawn.

As they neared the land of Tiponi's people, Shiye began leaving Dianna for hours at a time. He would leap ahead, looking for scouts, checking for danger.

"We'll have to come across the river, here," Shiye pointed at a roughly drawn map in the dirt beneath a leafless oak. "Tiponi's people are vigilant. There will be tribesmen watching the area from every available high point. If we're to find the place Matchitehew has indicated, we must do so in stealth."

Dianna nodded. "What will we do when we find him? Shiye, we need help. He could have a knife to Rose's neck as we speak."

Shiye sat back on his heels. Silence as thick as the snow on the ground surrounded them. There was no chirp of a bird, no rustlings of animals in the underbrush. Their breath rose in steam before their faces as they contemplated their next move. They were so close.

Dianna knew she was right in assuming Matchitehew hoped for them to witness the death of their daughter. Wanted them to see the life drain from her hazel eyes. She shivered.

"The medicine man," breathed Shiye suddenly. His eyes had opened wide. "Yahto. The man who sent his son to save me when I was to be executed. The medicine man in Tiponi's tribe. Perhaps, if we can get a message to him, he could help."

Dianna's brow creased in confusion. "How could we possibly get a message to him?"

Shiye was evidently thinking hard. "There's a place," he whispered. "Each day, Yahto will go into the forest alone. He sits in a small clearing to listen to the sounds of the trees around him. If we can watch the place, we might be able to convince him to help us."

Dianna stared at him. "That's a very slim chance, Shiye," she muttered so quietly that her husband had to lean forward to hear her as her chest rose and fell with the sound of her voice. It felt as though the very air around them was listening in on their conversation.

Shiye's gloved hand found Dianna's fingers and gave them a squeeze. "I don't see what other choice we have, Di. We can't do this alone."

Dianna's heart fluttered with panic, but her mind was clearer than it had ever been. She nodded.

It was a small clearing, covered with fresh, sparkling snow. In the middle there was a raised mound, indicating a rock or a fallen log. Dianna was relieved to see there were no footprints on the ground around the clearing. The medicine man of Tiponi's tribe had not yet come for his daily contemplation.

"I don't like this, Shiye," hissed Dianna, coming right up behind her husband as he crouched on the ground beneath the shelter of a tree. His eyes were fixed on the mound in the center of the clearing. "How do we know we can trust him?"

Shiye opened his mouth to respond, but a sound from behind the pair caused a jolt of surprise and fear to sear its way over her skin.

"I must ask," said a thick, rasping voice. "How I know I can trust you?"

Dianna whirled around, tripping over her filthy, damp skirts in shock. Shiye stood too, reaching for the knife in his belt, but the old man before them was smiling sadly. He looked ancient. The wrinkles in his dark skin appeared as though they had been carved into weathered wood. He was leaning heavily on a crooked walking stick carved with symbols Dianna didn't know the name of. His thin hair had been shaved down on one side of his head, but the other half was loose and long, fluttering in the slight morning breeze.

"Shiye," he said in a thick accent. "Háu, Mitakuyepi. It been long time."

"Yahto," said Shiye, lowering his blade. "Háu, Mitakuyepi."

The three observed one another for a few moments, and then Yahto said something quick and indecipherable to Shiye and Dianna listened as her husband answered curtly.

"He says he didn't think I would make it this long," said Shiye to Dianna, taking hold of her hand. Yahto smiled.

"And this is your woman?" he asked, raising his eyebrows at Shiye.

Shiye nodded. "My wife, Dianna." The muddy hem of Dianna's dress swung uncomfortably against her legs as Shiye urged her forward.

"Why have you returned here?" asked Yahto, sparing less than a glance in Dianna's direction.

Shiye hesitated, and then looked the older man straight in the eye. "Matchitehew has taken our child."

"There is nothing I can do for you," grumbled Yahto at once. His thick furs made him look enormous as he waved a dismissive hand and made to turn away.

"Please!" Dianna cried, reaching out to stop him. She hadn't meant to speak so loudly. "Please help us."

The old man sighed, his back still to them. "I have tried many time to help Shiye. I have tried to tell Kuckunniwi of the evil of his daughter, Tiponi. He will not see it. More have died in her name. More will die by her hand." He shook his head and gave another throaty sigh. "Perhaps Matchitehew will take a life and then be satisfied. Perhaps he will not."

Dianna let out a sob and Shiye straightened, anger coloring his features.

"You think our daughter's life is sufficient repayment, do you?! You think my crimes are so great so as to deserve this?"

Yahto's shoulders heaved in yet another sigh, and he shook his head. Dianna watched a number of feathers swinging from side to side in his hair with the movement. "Matchitehew will not be reasoned with. He would have to hear it from Tiponi's own lips before believing she was capable of murder his daughter."

"Then let us hear her confess," growled Shiye.

Yahto spun back to them, his lips pursed in thought. He looked very like a wrinkled old tortoise.

Dianna cast Shiye a stunned look. She didn't understand how he intended to force Tiponi's confession, but she could see the cogs working behind his eyes.

He had a plan.

Chapter Twelve

....

Now he waited. The girl played by the riverbank. It had been almost too easy to coerce the coward's daughter to accompany him away from her family, but she had caused enough difficulties on the journey to make up for it. She begged constantly for her parents, crying continuously until he subdued her with food or play.

"Will we reach home very soon?" she asked him for the thousandth time, skipping over to the place where he sat on a nearby rock.

Matchitehew's friendly composure slipped and he longed to seize the girl and throttle her on the spot.

"I have told you," he growled, so threateningly that she took a few steps away from him. "Your parents are coming to us here. They will be here soon. We must wait."

"Why must they meet us here?" asked Rose, her round eyes betraying a flicker of fear at his forceful reaction. Her hands, which held a large eagle feather she had found on their journey, dropped to her sides.

Matchitehew coaxed his expression into something that resembled kindness, although his heart was pounding in fury. He glanced at the place a short distance away from them. A spot on the ground that drew his eyes in a way he could not control. He could not fight the flood of emotion that invaded his soul, standing so close to this spot. He could see it more clearly than he did every night when he closed his eyes, more clearly than he had seen it in almost seven years.

Bena had lain there—his beautiful little girl—her dark hair matted with blood, her eyes closed. Tiponi had shrieked that Shiye was the one responsible, and his heart had been set on revenge from that very moment. He would make the wretch pay for this. He would rip out his heart.

Matchitehew smiled down at Shiye's weakness, at his foolishness. The embodiment of his revenge stood before him, looking up at him with innocent eyes. He did not answer her. He merely held a dirty-nailed finger to his lips.

"We must wait quietly now."

He was struck anew by how young she was. A small voice in the back of his mind murmured that the murder of an innocent was a terrible blemish upon his soul. That she was too young to understand, too precious to know, and free of the blame of her father's crimes.

But killing her was the only way he could repay Shiye for his sins. The only way he would make that man feel as he felt. As though his heart had been ripped from his very chest and lay beating on the ground in the frozen snow and mud.

She turned from him, her expression miserable, and he saw her little shoulders shiver with cold. His heart did not ache for her, he told himself. Soon she would lay where Bena had. Soon she would not feel cold. Or indeed feel anything ever again...

His resolution trembled. The little good left inside him whispered admonitions. He stood and went to retrieve a blanket from their horse's saddle.

"Couldn't we start a fire?" asked the girl, several hours later. "To be warmer?"

Matchitehew shook his head. "We're very nearly done waiting," he whispered. He cast a sidelong look at her. Her small arms were wrapped in the thick fur of the blanket he had handed her but she still shook with cold. The sun was beginning to set. *They should be here by now.*

It was another hour still when his ears finally pricked at the sound of voices. Loud, angry voices, arguing close by, muffled by the trees and the snow. If this was Shiye and his woman, they certainly weren't troubling to mask their presence. He glanced again at the little girl beside him. She had fallen asleep. Her dark hair fell into her round face in waves that rippled with the rhythm of her breathing like the surface of a clear pond. His resolution trembled worse than ever. The vengeful beast inside of him screamed for blood. The man in him still hesitated at the thought of the slaughter of a child. Even for a purpose such as his. But then he saw Bena, splayed on the ground, blood dripping from the gaping wound in her head. His abhorrence returned with ferocity and he launched himself to his feet, moving in the direction of the vehement shrieks he could hear a short distance away.

....

This was their only chance.

"Come alone," Yahto had told her. "Come meet me in the trees by the river. There are things we must discuss as your leadership moves forward."

Yes. They were counting on Tiponi's vanity to bring her to this place.

She had long-since married, according to Yahto, a man that sniveled and catered to her every outburst. His name was Hassun. He had once been a warrior, one of the most unmerciful men in the tribe. Now he seemed to exist only to do his wife's bidding. He cherished her, as enchanted by her as her father.

Yahto believed there were others in the tribe that understood Tiponi's cruelty. But the tightly woven group of faithful warriors around Kuckunniwi would not hear a word against the woman. This was how she maintained her position of power within her people. With the threat of harsh punishment to anyone who spoke out against her.

She was tyrannical. Little by little she was altering the sacred ways of the tribe. Changing old stories to suit her needs and punishing those who protested with banishment and worse.

"It would seem that the great spirits are watching over me," Yahto had mused as he told Shiye these things. "For, I should have long time ago, fallen prey to her rage. Perhaps she not want to meddle with the will of the Creator. Perhaps she fear him," he shrugged and sighed in his weary way. "She should fear him. I not think he will be pleased, knowing the things she has done."

And so they waited.

Dianna, crouching down in the underbrush beside Shiye, watched as Yahto's feet crunched anxiously over the frozen ground. It was freezing. Her teeth were chattering, not only with the cold but with nerves.

She had heard a lot about the woman behind Shiye's downfall. She had hated her for it. She hated her now. Her insides were roiling as though they had been filled with live snakes. She glanced up at Shiye.

His handsome face was taught with tension. He looked like a lion readying itself to pounce upon an unsuspecting prey. His hazel eyes were darker than usual in the dim, gray light of the winter sundown and Dianna was reminded again of his warrior heritage.

His high cheekbones were pale and bloodless in his dark skin. His jaw was set. He looked utterly terrifying.

She laid a tender hand on the back of his and he jerked away from her. Dianna flinched too, as though his rejection were a physical blow. Shiye looked down at her, and the hard lines of his face dissolved for a moment, giving her a glimpse of the love and the terror that filled his heart. He bent forward and pressed his frozen lips to hers.

"I love you," he whispered. His warm breath fluttered over her mouth and cheeks as he rained more silent kisses over her face. "I will always love you. I will protect you from harm all the days that I live, and I will love you long after I'm gone."

Dianna held in a sob as her eyes filled slowly with tears. These were the words he had said to her when he found out she was pregnant with Little Rose. He had spoken of both of them. Her and their unborn child, and Dianna knew that he spoke of them both now. "I know you will," she breathed. She took hold of her husband's face and pulled him to her.

Now she could feel his warmth. The heat in him that made him like sunlight, like joy, and yearning, and fire. She tasted him. Forgot the danger and the terror for a fraction of a second, and felt her love for this man pool in her chest like molten metal. He was a part of her. He was an iron casing around her heart, the armor that made her strong.

They pulled away from one another, the air in their lungs colliding in a mist between them, dancing around their cold, entwined fingers. Shiye held her for a moment longer, his forehead resting against hers, then he turned back to the empty space before them. The place where Yahto paced, wringing his aged fingers in front of his stomach as though he were trying to pull water from a sponge.

He was muttering to himself, his eyes darting around through the trees. Dianna settled back on her heels next to Shiye. They waited.

The sound of crunching footsteps soon reached them. It was a hesitant, exploratory sound, as though the person who approached them was wary of danger.

"Yahto?"

Tiponi stepped into the clearing, and a shard of ice slid down Dianna's throat and dropped into her belly. It settled in the pit of her stomach and caused her mouth to pull down in an expression of disgust.

She was beautiful. Of course, she was beautiful. Tiponi was tall. Her long, black hair swung freely, billowing out from her face and dangling below the fox fur she wore around her neck as a scarf. She had wide cheekbones and large, doe-like eyes that made her look repulsively innocent. Her lips were full and broad and, at the moment, they quirked up curiously on one side as she masticated a path through the snow towards Yahto.

Yahto faced her, his wrinkled skin a shade or two darker than hers, which was the color of caramel mixed with butter, and just as smooth. Dianna could feel a corrosive hate towards the woman building in her like gunpowder. All it needed was a spark to set it aflame. Jealousy reared its ugly head in Dianna's heart. This beautiful woman had, once, been engaged to marry Shiye. Would have shared his life, bore his children...

Shiye's hand came down on hers, and Dianna let out the breath she hadn't realized she'd been holding. Her husband's warm fingers wrapped themselves around her own, and when she looked at him, his handsome jaw was set. He nodded. Together, they turned back to watch the conversation taking place before them in the light of the dying sun.

Tiponi spoke sweetly to the medicine man as she came nearer, her doe-eyes wide and free of the madness Dianna associated with her name. Dianna struggled to make out what Tiponi was saying to Yahto. She was a little slow to understand and speak her husband's mother-tongue, and she despised the way the beautiful language sounded coming from the woman's mouth.

"Why should we have met here, of all places?" Tiponi asked, her tone dripping with honey. She came to a stop in front of Yahto and looked around at the surrounding trees.

"I thought it better that we were not overheard," muttered Yahto. He looked older than ever in the pale light of the evening. His wrinkles deepened with the coming shadows. "I know you seek to become the leader of the tribe. I am anxious to give you my support."

Tiponi let out a high, girlish laugh that didn't quite suit her. She looked like a grinning jungle cat, masking its teeth and claws as it snuggled closely to its victim.

"Your support? Do not kid me, Yahto. If there was ever a man more outspoken against the tides of change, I have not met him."

Yahto shrugged, the heavy furs girding his shoulders rising and swaying with the movement. "Perhaps the tides have changed without my help."

Tiponi looked as though she was repressing a snort with difficulty. "My father will never give me control of the tribe," she said in a soft voice that did not conceal her disregard for her father.

"But you do want it, don't you?" muttered Yahto. He shifted his weight from foot to foot and glanced back at the trees that concealed Shiye and Dianna from view.

"Want it?!" Tiponi shrieked, her high brows flying upwards. "There are so many things we could do differently. I could change so much. We needn't bow to the world around us. We could take it by the throat," she clenched her hand in the air before her, as though reaching to strangle an enemy. "Of course I want it," she breathed with venom.

Dianna was watching Tiponi's eyes. As she spoke, they lit with a crazed enthusiasm. Her hands fell and balled into fists at her sides.

Yahto had his back to them once more and Dianna could see his tension in the rigid way he held his tired bones. The walking stick in his hand seemed to be carrying more of his weight than his own feet. "But," he hesitated, suddenly sounding amused. "What good would come of this? A murderer is not usually the best choice for a leader. More the opposite."

Tiponi's beautiful face paled in the evening light. The snow around them glimmered as the sun began to fall behind the line of trees. Tiponi's eyes glinted. The corner of her mouth pulled up in a sneer. "Murderer?" she scoffed, trying to sound nonchalant. She swept a strand of long, black hair away from her face. "What nonsense is this?"

Shiye straightened at these words, the fading light illuminating his dark eyes, which were fixed on Tiponi like a bird of prey.

As he stepped forward, Dianna followed. Her daughter's face flitted into her mind as she faced the woman who had brought this horror upon them. *Lord, protect Rose. Let him come. Let this work. Protect her.*

Tiponi's whole aspect changed at once. She went still, like a wolf scenting its prey, and her full lips split in a malevolent grin.

"Shiye," she breathed. Her black eyes danced in the pressing shadows. "So, you have returned. And look," she gestured to Dianna, "you have brought a white harlot with you."

Shiye's chest inflated with fury. He took another step forward, but Dianna reached for him. He didn't look at her but he stopped in his tracks, breathing heavily. His nostrils flared.

Dianna was shivering. The damp snow had long-since soaked the hem of her dress and her fingers were numb with cold.

"Does she have you on a leash, dear one?" cooed Tiponi, eyeing Dianna's hand on Shiye's forearm. She had taken a step back from the three that stood facing her. "Have you come back to try again to take my life? Was the life of the child not enough?"

"Bena's death was not by my hand," Shiye snarled. He took another measured step. Her doe-eyes gazed innocently across the space between them, without fear. She was daring him to come nearer, excited by the challenge.

"It is your word against mine, Shiye, as it has always been," Tiponi's smile widened, showing yellowed teeth. Her eyes darted to Dianna and slid over her tattered dress in a way that suggested she was sizing her up, appraising her possibilities.

"Does your pretty one know you are a murderer?" she whispered conspiratorially, holding a hand to her lips in mock-secrecy.

"Does your father know you seek to usurp him?" spat Shiye.

Tiponi laughed. "My father would not recognize that kind of ambition in a woman." She moved away from them, attempting to slide back into the shelter of the trees. "

Yahto intervened. "I saw Bena die," he said loudly. His hands were wrapped around his walking stick, his arms trembling. With cold or with anxiety, Dianna couldn't tell.

"I was at the river that day," his shaking voice rasped.

Shiye spun around so quickly that he flung snow in all directions with his haste. "Why?" he asked Yahto. "Why have you not said anything? Spoke to Kuckunniwi?"

"I have, Shiye," said Yahto, sadly. "But I must confess that my opinion is counting for less and less every day with Kuckunniwi. Tiponi's doing, of course."

Tiponi, Dianna saw, was grinning again. "The visions of a madman are worth very little amongst our people," she purred, twirling a finger coyly through her black hair. She gave a soft wink and turned away from the three of them. "I would run, Shiye. If I were you. The warriors will be after you the moment I inform them of your presence."

Shiye lost control. Dodging around Dianna's outstretched fingers, he reached Tiponi in three strides and seized hold of her arm. Tiponi screamed. Screamed so loudly that Dianna had to resist the urge to rush forward and cover the woman's lips with her hand.

Shiye was shaking her. "Confess!" he yelled into Tiponi's face. "Confess to your crimes!"

"To whom?!" shrieked Tiponi through a new peal of laughter. "To you?! We both know the truth Shiye. The brat was clumsy. Worthless. She deserved her death."

Shiye let out a howl of fury and threw Tiponi from him. She landed in the snow in a heap, still laughing. "What could you possibly have gained by coming here?! Run, Shiye. Run away. Far away!" Her laughter was a terrifying thing to witness. This was her madness. Her doe-eyes were glassy with unshed tears of joy, her complexion flushed with the pleasure of her victory. "They are coming for you," she cackled. "They'll have heard my scream. They are coming for you."

Dianna didn't know where her lapse in control came from. The fury and pain welling inside her burst their bounds like the destruction of a dam. She wasn't aware of deciding to approach Tiponi, but she was suddenly there, bending low to yank the laughing woman to her feet as she continued to screech her pleasure to the stars.

Unaware of what she was doing, she pulled back her fist and slammed it into the woman's face. Her maniacal laughter ceased abruptly. Tiponi clutched her jaw, looking up at Dianna in bewilderment as Dianna's second fist connected with her stomach.

Dianna had never struck anyone as hard as she did Tiponi. Never felt such utter contempt and violence towards another human being in all her life.

She heard Shiye yelling her name as she lifted Tiponi by her black hair and pulled her bleeding knuckles back for the third time.

"Confess," she spat. "You were the one to kill Bena, weren't you? It was you. Not Shiye. Not my husband."

"Of course it was me!" Tiponi's mad eyes were dancing with glee at Dianna's attack. "I shoved the brat and she fell. Down, down, down!" She sang the last three words through a bubble of blood at the corner of her lips. "Her blood spilled into the river. It washed down the stream! It was me! I took her life. And now she is one less weakling to coddle and tend. One less useless, worthless mouth to feed!"

Something hit Dianna with the force of a stampeding bull. She was thrown backward, away from Tiponi, and landed splay-legged against a nearby tree.

Snow tumbled down from its branches around her and, for a moment, she couldn't see what was happening in the space beyond.

There were the sounds of a scuffle, shouts, and a thud. Dianna saw Tiponi clamber to her feet and skitter away into the trees. A tall, dark figure darted after her. Tiponi's singsong voice wove back to them on the wind, a stream of curses trailed from the mouth of the man who chased her.

"Shiye?" Dianna called, sitting up.

"Di?" Shiye was climbing to his feet a short distance away.

"Was that him?"

Shiye nodded as he lifted Dianna to a standing position and took hold of her hand. "Come," he said, and they followed the dancing figures of Tiponi and Matchitehew as they raced through the trees. They were running flat out, chasing the sound of shrieking laughter that emanated from the space ahead of them. The rushing sound of the nearby river grew louder with every step. An opening appeared in the trees ahead. There came a startled shriek, a bellowed oath, and then a final, long, drawn-out scream. Silence except for the flow of water.

Chapter Thirteen

Shiye and Dianna skidded to a stop beside the hulking figure of an Indian man. He was looking down at the long drop to the river below.

"She ran right off the edge," he growled. "Still laughing." Dianna was startled at the English words that fell from Matchitehew's lips.

"Oh my," Dianna whispered. The man looked at her. He smelled. His face was grimy, his teeth were yellow, and he looked about ready to toss Dianna off the cliff as well. Shiye stepped between them.

"I have waited for this day for seven years," Matchitehew grumbled to Shiye, looking up at him. "I would have hunted you and your child until to the ends of the Earth to repay you for the murder of my own."

"Where is she?" squeaked Dianna, louder than she'd intended. Stepping around her husband to grasp the cloth covering Matchitehew's arm. "Where is our daughter?"

"Mama?" Rose's voice drifted out from the shadow of the trees. All three of them looked up at the sound.

"Rose?!" yelled Dianna and Shiye at the same time. Flinging herself across the distance that separated them, Dianna yanked her daughter into her arms in a hug that stole her breath. She began to sob. Shiye collapsed on the ground next to them, his shoulders heaving as he held his daughter's angelic face in his massive hands.

"Rose," he whispered, relief punctuating every breath. "Rose."

Dianna was kissing every part of her child that she could reach. Rose was shivering, her dress was wet. Her dark hair was plastered to her face, and her creamy, freckled cheeks were red with cold. Dianna clung to her, still sobbing, unable to control herself. *Oh, thank you. Thank you, Lord. Thank you.* Her breath was coming in shuddering gasps. She felt she could have sat there and held her daughter to her chest for a million, undisturbed hours.

The sound of a throat clearing behind them made Dianna look up, wiping tears from her eyes. Yahto stood there against the dark backdrop of the forest, and at his back, several armed Indians had drawn their bows. They were pointing them directly at Shiye's chest.

"No!" cried Dianna, leaping to her feet. She shoved Rose behind her back and stepped forward. Her arms held out. Shiye shoved her out of harm's way. The hands on the bowstrings tensed, and Shiye held up his hands in a gesture of surrender.

"Please," he said, "we mean no harm."

Yahto opened his mouth to speak, but...

"I have heard a confession," said a rough voice from the river's edge, "from the murderer of my child." Matchitehew moved into the shaft of moonlight illuminating Dianna's husband. One by one, the men lowered their bows, their eyes fixed on Matchitehew's heavy-jawed face. "Shiye is innocent of the crime Tiponi accused him of so many years ago," he said, casting a miserable stare around at the watching Indians. He was silent for a moment, his massive shoulders slumped and weary. "Tiponi was the one responsible for Bena's death."

The men around them all drew breath as one, looking around at one another and then down at Yahto, who nodded gravely. The last hand that gripped an arrow fell.

"What has happened here, Matchitehew?"

Matchitehew cleared his throat uncomfortably, casting a nervous glance down at Rose's face. Rose was looking confused at the incomprehensible conversation taking place around her. Shiye stepped up beside Matchitehew.

"I have returned to right the many wrongs against my name," he said.

The warriors shifted agitatedly. Dianna saw fists tightened, eyes narrow. Shiye and Tiponi's tribes had been warring for so long, that his very appearance was a threat, whether he was innocent or not.

There came a shifting behind the warriors and they all separated to let a tall, broad-shouldered man come to the fore of the group.

"You speak ill against my wife," he growled, his lips thin and his eyes narrowed to dangerous slits above a wide, flat nose. "What have you done with her?"

Matchitehew looked over his shoulder in the darkness. "She has thrown herself to the river," he said, at last, gesturing to the cliff. "She confessed to Bena's murder, and when I gave chase, she leapt off the edge."

"No," hissed the man. He ran forward, shoved roughly past Matchitehew, and fell to his knees, staring down into the black chasm of the river below.

"It is no good, Hassun," said Matchitehew to Tiponi's distraught husband. "She is gone."

"No," Hassun muttered again. "Tiponi!!" His huge hands grasped the icy rocks around ledge as he raged his wife's name into the darkness. Begging for her to surface. But the water was too cold. The river, too fast. The drop, too far. Tiponi would have been killed by the fall. She would not have survived. The others were silent.

Most of the warriors gathered around them looked outraged at the news. A few looked unhinged, but a small handful appeared slightly relieved.

Yahto stepped forward. "Come," he said, gesturing to Dianna, Shiye, Rose and Matchitehew. All of whom cast him doubtful, appraising looks. "We must speak to Kuckunniwi. We must tell him what has become of his daughter."

The walk through the icy night was not pleasant. With her daughter safe at last, all of the energy seemed to have left Dianna's body, so that it was all she could do to clutch Little Rose's hand and keep moving forward through the snow. They reached Kuckunniwi's camp in within a half an hour, their bodies aching and worn. Dianna feeling she might soon collapse from exhaustion.

Shiye now carried Rose, who had fallen asleep on his shoulder. Matchitehew trailed behind them, his eyes downcast. Dianna wondered what he was feeling. Shame? Fury? Sadness?

They entered the camp accompanied by a flurry of snow and movement. A fire glimmered in the center of a haphazard arrangement of dwellings and tents. Three men stood before the flames. As they approached, Little Rose awoke and slid from her father's arms to walk alongside Dianna.

One of the men Dianna recognized from the clifftop overhanging the river. He must have run ahead to alert the chief of their approach. She felt a chill creep down her spine as the tallest man of the three spun to face them. His hair too was long and black. It fell down his back in a long plait. His face was lined, furious, and etched with an incomprehensible misery.

"So," he said in English, as their motley crew drew closer to the heat of the blazing fire. "I am told you have come to inform me of the death of my daughter, Tiponi."

This then was Kuckunniwi. The man that her husband loathed for his inability to see the truth. The man who had allowed Matchitehew to hunt them, and helped him do so, in the beginning.

"Her death is no tragedy," growled Matchitehew suddenly. He shoved himself forward so that he stood inches away from his chief, staring at him with heartbroken fury in his voice. "I heard her confession from her very lips. She laughed—" Matchitehew's voice broke. "Tiponi laughed as she spoke of murdering Bena. My little one."

Kuckunniwi's eyes opened wide. "Tiponi could not have committed such a crime," he growled. "How dare you suggest—"

Yahto spoke from behind Matchitehew. "I have tried to tell you for years, Kuckunniwi. I have tried to make you see it."

Kuckunniwi shook his head, staring passed Matchitehew. His coal black eyes fixed on Rose.

"Who is this?" he muttered, confusedly. "Whose child is this? Why is she here?"

Shiye stepped around Yahto so that the firelight fell on his face.

"You!" Kuckunniwi cried, shocked. He reeled backward, nearly landing himself in the fire. "Why is this man still standing?" he bellowed. "I will cut out his heart for daring to return here."

"Kuckunniwi, listen to me," sighed Yahto. His shoulders sagged, he looked just as exhausted as Dianna felt.

At that moment, a young man approached the group. Rising out of the darkness like a ghost, he stepped forward to grip Yahto's shoulder.

"I've been searching for you, Father. What is going on?" The young man's eyes skated over the many faces turned towards him and fell on Shiye. He smiled.

"So," he said, taking another step. "You've returned."

"Delsin," said Shiye in greeting. The two men came forward and embraced like brothers.

"Delsin and his father are the reason I still breathe on this day," Shiye explained to Dianna, indicating Yahto. "It was Delsin who aided me in my escape the day I was to die for Tiponi's crime. Delsin, this is my wife, Dianna."

Dianna offered Delsin a tired smile in greeting and he nodded before turning back to his father.

"What is going on?"

Haltingly, and with many wheezing pauses in between, Yahto began to tell the story. He started on the day several years previously, when Matchitehew's daughter was killed.

"I had gone to the river in search of Tiponi, for her father had need of her. I came upon them as they stood by the water. Tiponi was shrieking. Angry about her broken beads. Angry about being forced to marry Shiye. Her tantrum was not a pleasant thing to see." Yahto paused here and met the eyes of every person in the circle. Dianna had a feeling they had all witnessed Tiponi's violent outbursts before now. "I heard her yelling that she would treat her people however she saw fit, and then I watched her shove Bena to the ground. When the child did not rise, I came directly to you, Kuckunniwii. I told you what I saw, and you dismissed me. Then Tiponi came tearing out of the trees. She was screaming that Shiye had tried to kill her. That Shiye had killed Bena. You heeded her."

Yahto was staring at his chief, but Kuckunniwii, Dianna was pleased to see, didn't seem to be able to meet the old man's eyes. Yahto exhaled violently, leaning on his walking stick, and shook his head.

"When you proclaimed that Shiye should die for Tiponi's misdeeds, I caused a scene, and Delsin went to Shiye to help free him.

"It has been years. I knew Matchitehew would never cease to hunt Shiye, but I did not understand his thirst for revenge would bring him to this point. They are all here tonight because Matchitehew intended to murder Shiye's daughter on the same spot, on the same day Bena was killed, at the same age that Bena died. He has been planning this night for a long time. It is a miracle that his plan did not succeed."

Matchitehew was pale in the firelight. He looked around, his face a mask of repentance as all eyes found him and fixed him where he stood.

"Mere words cannot express my remorse," he grumbled in his deep voice. His eyes slid to Shiye. "I will tell you, that at the end...." he paused. "I do not think I could have taken your child's life."

Shiye scowled at him. "The idea that you considered it is repugnant," he seethed. "I will not grant you my forgiveness."

"I cannot ask for it." Matchitehew straightened his shoulders as he looked Shiye directly in the eye. "I will make amends to you as long as I live. I will give your family my life. With what is left of my honor, I will protect them until my dying breath."

Dianna raised her eyebrows at her husband, who frowned, and shook his dark head. "I do not think—"

"It is not a question, Shiye. I owe your family more than my body and spirit for the hurt I have inflicted upon them."

Dianna watched Shiye's reaction. He examined the man before him with a calculated gaze. After a moment, he nodded. Matchitehew's wide mouth parted in a sorrowful grimace of thanks. His eyes fell onto Little Rose, who stood gripping Dianna's filthy skirts; her round cheeks still rosy with cold and exhaustion.

"I am sorry, Rose," he whispered.

Dianna felt a sudden chill make its way down her spine that had nothing to do with the snow. She eyed Matchitehew's face. The face that had haunted her nightmares, tormented her every waking thought for months.

Somehow, though, without his malevolent grin, he was less frightening. He looked, in Dianna's opinion, like a man that did not know where he was or what to do. While he could not be older than forty years, his worn visage made him look like a man of sixty; and his scraggly, dust-covered hair put her in mind of a drunkard she had once seen sitting on a street corner in Manhattan. That man too had looked worn, exhausted, and heartbroken.

His appearance did not change the fact that he had threatened her daughter's life. Any man that could lower himself to such an act would not be welcomed near her family.

Rose, however, did not seem to be thinking along these lines. The exhausted little girl had released Dianna's skirts and tottered across the way to stare up into Matchitehew's face.

Dianna had to fight back the urge to yell and yank her daughter away. Rose stared up at Matchitehew for so long that the other members of the circle began to shift uncomfortably. Shiye cleared his throat.

Rose glanced at her father and then reached for Matchitehew's hand.

"Chew would never hurt me, Papa. I told you. He kept me safe all the way here. He kept me warm while we waited for you to meet us."

Dianna felt tears begin sliding down her cold cheeks. She didn't know how to feel or what to say. She could only watch as her daughter stood on her tiptoes to press a kiss to Matchitehew's grimy, whiskery cheek.

Chapter Fourteen

Shiye was holding his breath as fury filtered into his stomach. He couldn't seem to help himself. Logically, he realized that Matchitehew no longer posed a threat to his daughter, but he could not banish the sick feeling of fear he felt as he watched Little Rose bestow a forgiving kiss on her long-time friend.

Chew. The nickname reminded him of the depth of Matchitehew's plot against him. The meticulous way he'd cultivated Rose for years. The unsavory act of violence he had intended against her. But Matchitehew was crying.

Tears of remorse were actually flooding down his face, trickling into the laces of his black shirt front. Shiye watched the man give his daughter an unwieldy pat on the head and then Dianna came forward to pull Rose away from him. Shiye let out his breath and turned back to Yahto, who continued his story with a nod in Shiye's direction.

"Shiye and his wife found me in the forest. Together, we hatched a plan to bring Tiponi and Matchitehew to the same place, so that Matchitehew might hear her confess and cease his plans to murder Rose. We could only hope to stage a disagreement and draw Matchitehew to us with the noise.

"I asked Tiponi to meet me under the guise of furthering her rise to power, and she came. She spoke of her desire to take control of the tribe. To move us into war. When Shiye and Dianna showed themselves, she spoke cruelly to them. She goaded Shiye and laughed in his face. Dianna forced a confession from her, and it was then that Matchitehew leaped from the trees and attacked her, for she showed every sign of being pleased with having murdered Bena."

Yahto forced his chief to meet his eyes. "Matchitehew spoke the truth, Kuckunniwii. I witnessed Tiponi's confession. She laughed as she spoke of his daughter's death."

Kuckunniwii looked shocked. His mouth had fallen open in a comical 'O.' His onyx eyes were wide.

"Tiponi fled and Matchitehew gave chase," Yahto continued. "I do not think she intended to leap from the cliff's edge. She would not have died so easily. She was too determined to rule over us all. In any case, she fell to the river from the high cliff. She will not have survived."

Shiye watched as Kuckunniwii swallowed. His eyes flashed around the circle. The two warriors standing beside him appeared sorrowful and lost.

"We shall restore the peace agreement," Kuckunniwii said, at last, clearing his throat. " He approached Shiye, who had to repress the urge to pull his blade on the man that had threatened him for so long. "You have my apologies," he muttered hoarsely. Shiye had repressed a snort with difficulty. His *apologies*. Kuckunniwi's watery eyes fell on Yahto. "And you, Yahto. I am sorry that I did not believe you."

Yahto bowed his head in acknowledgment. "It is not an easy thing for a father to believe there is an evil in their child," he whispered.

Kuckunniwii nodded gravely, his eyes filling with sudden tears. "We will go to search for Tiponi's body," he said to his warriors. "I will give you shelter this night," he said to Shiye and Dianna.

Shiye nodded. Kuckunniwii turned to walk away but then at the last second, he spun back around. His tear-filled eyes fixed on Little Rose, who was nodding to sleep against Dianna's hip.

"Your daughter is very beautiful," he murmured.

With that, Kuckunniwii disappeared into the night, his long furs swaying behind him as he walked.

One of Kuckunniwi's men trailed after him, while the other remained behind.

"If you come with me," he growled, looking none-to-friendly. "I'll take you to your beds."

Shiye glowered at the man, who returned his look with interest. Despite Kuckunniwi's reassurances, Shiye did not feel safe surrounded by these people.

Chief Kuckunniwi's people called themselves the Nahkote`, and the history between their tribe and Shiye's was a long and bloody one. He flinched at the slightest crack of a twig coming from the trees, and herded his family before him with his hand on the long handle of his hunting knife. The elk horn handle felt comforting in his palm.

To his dismay, Matchitehew trailed after them. They stopped before the wide mouth of a cave opening a hundred yards away from the fire. A deerskin cloth was fixed over the cave entrance, giving the illusion of privacy to the occupants.

"You will sleep here," said the man leading them as he drew to a halt. He pointed to the cave entrance, nodded to Matchitehew, and then walked away. Shiye cast a wary glance over his shoulder at Matchitehew. His expression was blank, unreadable. Shiye couldn't help think that, even though his innocence had been confirmed, Matchitehew would still rather dispatch Shiye then protect him. A hundred years of animosity and bloodshed was not forgotten in either of their minds.

It had been the same when Shiye had first come to live with the Nahkoté after it was decided that he and Tiponi would be married. They had tolerated his presence because their chief had instructed them to do so, but given the choice, they would rather see him scalped, if for no other reason than that he was a member of their enemy tribe.

Shiye peered into the cave and, seeing no sign of danger, he held the cloth aside so that his family could enter. Matchitehew, true to his word, planted himself firmly outside of the opening, facing the dark night and the blazing fire in the distance. He caught Shiye's eye as he made to walk by him. They exchanged a nod, and Shiye understood that Matchitehew did not mean to sleep. He would keep watch outside the cave and alert Shiye at the merest hint of danger. A cacophony of emotions gambled around inside his head as he settled down beside his wife and daughter, neither of whom were speaking much. They were both exhausted and shivering with cold.

The cave held a selection of musty fur blankets, and Shiye was reminded forcibly of the days when he had first met Dianna. Her golden hair shone in the darkness of the cave, and though his eyes were heavier than they had ever been, he couldn't stop looking at her. He watched as Dianna bundled Rose into the bed of furs, and his heart throbbed. His. They were his. For the moment, Shiye thought, glancing at the cave entrance, where he could just make out the outline of Matchitehew standing sentinel outside the door, they were safe. Truly safe. The reason for which he had been hunted had been finally been abolished. Matchitehew hunted them no more. Not a soul would hunt them now. When the dawn came, they would find their horses and head for home.

His heart gave another dull throb as he settled down beside his wife and child, caressing their faces.

Dianna opened bleary eyes and smiled drowsily up at him. "We're safe?" she whispered as Rose began to snore softly.

"For now," he said, casting another uneasy glance at the figure outside the door. Dianna followed his gaze and Shiye saw her shiver. But there was nothing they could do about Matchitehew's presence except to let him prove himself out. Shiye didn't think he would be able to sleep. He bent forward and pressed his lips to Dianna's. He breathed in the scent of her and laughed.

"We need a bath," he chuckled.

Dianna looked affronted and then she laughed too.

"I'll accomplish that just as soon as Winter fades," she said. "I doubt I shall wake until then."

Shiye shook his head with a smile and pulled his family close in the darkness. Bestowing many small kisses over his daughter's sleeping face, he wrapped them in his arms and glared protectively towards the cave entrance. Determined to keep watch on them as they slept.

The dawn found him snoring. As much as he had been bent on staying awake the whole night through, there were some things even an obstinate Indian man could not fight. Weeks of little to no sleep had left him weak and exhausted, but with Rose back in his arms, his resilience had failed. His body had relaxed against his will and he had fallen into a coma-like state.

He did not wake as the clan gradually came to life outside the cave. It was afternoon before the stirrings of his wife and child caused him to come abruptly alert. He sat up, staring around the cave.

"Papa," said Rose, approaching him immediately. "Are you hungry? Chew brought us some food."

Suddenly ravenous, Shiye took the cold hunk of corn bread from his daughter's fingers and tore it into two. He offered the second half to her as he bit into the first, but Rose shook her head.

"I already had lot's," she said cheerfully, pointing at a stone bowl on the floor by her mother's feet.

Dianna was sitting near his feet, her back propped against the stone wall of the cave. She looked beautiful in the half-light. Her golden hair, silhouetted with dim sunshine, made her look as though she were wearing a halo. Although she still appeared to have been rolled through mud and left out to dry, she was smiling.

Shiye imagined that he too looked much the worse for wear. He glanced over at Rose, who was watching him with a satisfied look on her face.

"It's good, huh?"

Shiye crammed the rest of the bread hungrily into his mouth and then reached playfully for his daughter. She squealed as he hauled her into his huge arms.

"You," he said, planting a kiss on the top of her head, "must tell me about your adventure. What happened, Rose? Did Matchitehew grab you when you were playing in the garden at your grandfather's house? Did he hurt you?"

Shiye ran his hands protectively over his daughter's arms, peering down into her sweet face, which suddenly looked sheepish. Evidently, she had hoped this point would come up later, if at all.

"I..." she hesitated, glancing up at her mother as Dianna scooted across the bedding to sit beside Shiye. Rose looked between them for a few moments and then, without warning, she burst into tears.

"There's nothing to cry about," said Dianna soothingly. "It's all right now, see? We're here. You're safe."

"I—I heard him call for me," Little Rose stuttered, casting a tear-filled eye to the cave entrance, where Matchitehew undoubtedly still sat. "Chew called for me."

Shiye felt his insides turn to ice.

"He always whistles," she said, "like a bird. He whistles, and that means it's time to sneak away to play."

"To sneak away?" asked Dianna, coolly. She looked up at Shiye and they exchanged a dark look.

"He would call when we were at home. He's always been there, Mama. I've always had Chew," Rose choked.

"What do you mean, always?" whispered Shiye.

"He would come when you were gone," Rose said through a hiccup. "He would come when you went away. He said he was sent to keep me company while my Papa made sure we were safe."

"Of course," Shiye said, smacking a hand to his forehead. "The traveler heading East. He would make a trail that led me on a merry chase, and then come back to you while I was gone."

He and Dianna exchanged terrified glances once more and then they both looked toward the cave opening.

"I was always so uneasy when you left. I watched Rose like a hawk. I don't see how she could have been meeting him in secret... How could I have missed—?"

"It was sometimes nighttime when he would come. Sometimes when you were in the kitchen and I was playing outside." Rose shrugged guiltily, tears still pouring down her face. "He is my friend, Papa. Please do not send him away." Rose buried her face in his shirt. He could feel her tears soaking into the material.

"Rose," he said sternly. "How could you think to keep something like this from us?"

"I didn't know it was bad, Papa. That was just the way it always was!"

Shiye sighed and combed his fingers through his long hair. He was met with matted tangles, and he desisted out of disgust. His hair was a symbol of life and happiness. He had never neglected it before. He would have shorn it off if he had lost his daughter, as a semblance of mourning. He made a mental note to wash it as soon as possible.

"Don't you ever keep secrets from us again, Rose. We are your Mama and Papa. We love you, and we need you to trust that we know what's best for you."

"I didn't know," sobbed Rose into his shirt. "Papa, I didn't know."

"He could have killed you, Rose, do you understand?"

Rose sat up, her eyes puffy and swollen and she looked at Shiye with an expression that told him she did not believe him. "He is my friend, Papa."

"Not anymore," said Shiye sternly.

Rose dissolved again into sobs.

Shiye left the cave in a fury and gestured to Matchitehew to follow him. He did so. Standing, and brushing dust from his canvas pants.

"You planted this in her," Shiye hissed. He gestured to the deerskin covered entrance of the cave. "You made her love you. Trust you."

Matchitehew wore an expression of utter self-loathing. He said nothing.

"She is a child!" Shiye shouted, losing his temper completely. "Child of a murderer or not, she is an innocent."

"I wanted to make you burn, as I did," muttered Matchitehew, scuffing the toe of his boot in the snow. "I saw the life you were trying to create, and I wanted to take it from you."

Shiye's hands dropped to his sides. He stared at the man before him with the utmost loathing, and then something clicked into place.

He imagined how he would feel if Rose was taken from him. If he came at the sound of shouts to find his daughter had been murdered. He imagined someone pointing the finger at a man, saying 'he is the cause of your pain' and he understood. His expression softened.

He took a step away from Matchitehew. "Revenge is a terrible thing to devote your life to, Matchitehew," he said simply because he could not disagree with the man. No, he did not think for a second that he would endanger an innocent child, but he knew why Matchitehew had done the things he'd done. He could not yet forgive him, but he could understand.

"I will spend all my days making amends for the wrong I have done to you and your family," he repeated.

Shiye nodded.

Chapter Fifteen

They left Kuckunniwi's people without a backward glance. Shiye had bid farewell to the Chief but been unable to say anything more. He was sorry the man had lost his daughter, but he was not sorry Tiponi was dead. He thought any words on the subject would sound empty and hollow coming from his lips. He wanted to say thank you for the kindness, but he could not honestly say this either. After the tribulation and turmoil Kuckunniwii had brought on him with his ignorance, Shiye felt he deserved as much as one hundred nights of kindness from the man.

The Chief of the Nahkoté let them depart with an air of being glad to see the back of them. The other tribesmen said nothing. Some glared. Others seemed to be beyond caring.

Yahto and his son, Delsin, met them a few hundred yards outside the camp. The snow was melting around them, dripping from the trees and glimmering in the unexpected glow of the late afternoon sun.

"I am glad to finally put this to rest," he said. Delsin nodded fervently.

"I have much to thank you for," Shiye said humbly. "My life is restored to me. My debt to you is great."

Yahto waved a wrinkled, quavering hand dismissively. "If you do right by another, you may consider your debt to us paid," he said.

Shiye nodded, clasped Yahto's forearm, and then he mounted his horse.

"We will see each other again?" he asked.

"Perhaps," said the old man. He smiled. "Take care of your loved ones, Shiye. They are your tribe, now."

Shiye's eyebrows lifted as he smiled. He tipped his wide-brimmed hat to Yahto, and then he set off into the trees. His wife, his daughter, and his worst enemy trailing after him with tired smiles of their own.

"Can't we go home first?" Shiye begged his wife. A few days of slow travel found them rounding Laramie Peak once more. The snow there was still thick on the ground and more had come in the night.

"I need to get a message to them as soon as I can, Shiye," said Dianna stubbornly. She turned in her saddle. "My family said they would follow us."

"Did you even tell them where to go?" Shiye grouched, pulling off his leather glove to scratch an itch beneath his left eye.

"Of course I did," Dianna snapped. She was just as tired as he was. Just as sick of being in the saddle. "They know to ride towards Buffalo Creek from Laramie Peak."

"I still can't imagine your mother on a horse," Shiye snorted with amusement.

Dianna's stern expression slid into a grin. "Nor can I," she admitted. Then she sighed. "I can't figure out how on Earth I'm going to fit all of this in a letter," she said, gesturing to the three horses and their riders.

Matchitehew smiled weakly. "It has been a rather unfortunate series of events," he said, idly. He cast an unsettled glance over his shoulder.

"Tell me," Dianna asked him, slowing her horse down so that she could ride alongside Matchitehew.

"How is it your English is so perfect? If you don't mind my asking."

Matchitehew looked over his shoulder again. Dianna ignored this, looking at him quizzically, waiting for him to respond. Shiye however, cast a nervous glance at the path behind them as well. He could tell that he and Matchitehew were experiencing the same creeping feeling. A feeling of unease, a prickling on the back of his neck. It felt like they were being followed.

His wife, however, seemed completely unaware, and for the moment, he thought it best to keep it that way.

"My mother was determined that the white settlers meant us no harm," Matchitehew was saying. He cast Dianna an appraising look. "She befriended a white woman from a ranch near our village and, over several years, learned her language back to front. She could even read it. She would come home with books and read them to me in English."

He shrugged. "I still like to read," he said. "I handled all the trade with the ranchers after my mother died. We used to trade with them for beef mostly. The owner's wife had a fondness for beadwork."

Dianna nodded. Little Rose, who was riding in front of her mother, smiled at Matchitehew. He winked at her. Then caught Shiye's eye and immediately became somber once more, assuming an expression that would have been appropriate at the bedside of a sick person.

"Hold it," Shiye said suddenly. He held up his left hand to signal the others to halt. He had spotted something out of place ahead; a strange darkness on the uninterrupted white of the snow on the path before them. His eyes traveled around the surrounding trees.

"Matchitehew," Shiye called. He listened to the snorting of Matchitehew's horse as Matchitehew pulled his steed up next to his. "Do you see what I see?" he asked, his eyes still combing the tree line. The ground on either side of them was slightly elevated and Shiye didn't like it. He liked having the high ground at all times.

"Go back or forward?" Matchitehew whispered to Shiye. He pulled a large hunting knife from its sheath on his hip. Shiye did the same. He turned to his wife.

"Do you have your knives?"

Dianna nodded looking scared. She bundled Rose into her chest and his daughter looked up at her mother, her eyes wide and fearful. "What is it, Mama?"

"I don't know."

Matchitehew had climbed from his horse's back and knelt to pick up the thing on the ground before them. As the soft strands caught the light, Dianna gasped.

"That's not... hair? Is it?"

Matchitehew nodded. "My best guess is that Tiponi's widower, Hassun, is not quite pleased with us at the present moment," he said. "In mourning, the Nahkoté will cut off their hair to display their respect for their lost loved one."

Shiye watched Dianna swallow. Then she nodded.

"Forward or back, Shiye?" asked Matchitehew. He dropped the clump of black hair back onto the snow, wiping his palm over his britches.

Shiye's mind was whirring. His eyes never left their surroundings. "I don't think it matters much," he growled, finally. "If he wants to attack us, he'll find a way to do it. Let's go on."

Matchitehew remounted his palomino horse and allowed Dianna and Rose to ride past him before directing the animal onto the path behind them. Shiye looked back at Matchitehew before they set off and their eyes met once more. It was in that moment, as Shiye took in the determined expression on the other man's face, that he understood the depth of Matchitehew's promise. He would defend Shiye's family until his last breath was drawn to make right the wrong of his past actions.

Shiye urged his horse forward through the now ominous silence of the forest, his knife held ready at his side and his senses on high alert. As they progressed, Shiye began feeling more and more like a rabbit caught in a snare. The ground on either side of them sloped steadily upwards, but just over the next hill, they would crest the highest point of the pass. He motioned to Dianna and Matchitehew and they pushed their horses into a gallop. He hoped they could cover the distance quickly, and gain some higher ground.

An arrow went whizzing in front of Shiye's face. So close that he felt the fletching sting the tip of his nose as it passed. He tossed his body low over his horse's neck and looked back over his shoulder. Dianna had curled herself around their daughter, shielding her from harm and kicked her horse faster.

A second arrow flew by his ear. Shiye, terrified for his wife and daughter's safety, slowed his horse and circled around beside them, trying to give them the added coverage of his body. The path was wide, they galloped side by side. The higher ground was falling away behind them now. They crested the hill, now sloping steeply downwards.

The third arrow caught Shiye in the shoulder. He cried out, and the pain of it caused his hand to slip on his horse's reins. He grappled with the leather, but his gloves made his fingers clumsy. The shifting of the horse beneath him was agonizing. Shiye felt his body tip sideways. He toppled and fell. His horse skittered to a halt as the reins were jerked out his fingers.

Dianna and Rose's steed turned sideways to avoid a collision and all was chaos.

A hulking figure leapt from the cover of the trees and Shiye felt the man land him a crushing blow to the diaphragm. Eyes stinging with pain, Shiye clutched at his stomach.

Another blow collided with the side of his head and Shiye rolled sideways to avoid a third, tearing the arrow out of his shoulder in the process. He let out a cry of agony. As he attempted to gain his feet, he saw another figure forcing Dianna from the back of her horse by the hair.

"Get away from them," he screamed. He had lost his senses. He was blind with panic. Then, out of nowhere, out of nothing, Matchitehew was there. In one swift motion, he dispatched the warrior facing Shiye and turned his blade on the other. The one who now held a knife to his wife's throat.

Little Rose had somehow managed to cling to the horse. She was shrieking for her mother, tears pouring down her face.

"She chose me!" Hassun screamed at Shiye, his hair was shorn to uneven lengths all over his head. "Tiponi was mine!"

"She used you," gasped Shiye, straightening up and seizing the handle of his second blade. He'd lost his first when he had fallen from his horse.

"She loved me!" Hassun's eyes were wild. He was deranged. Flecks of spit flew from his wide mouth and hit Dianna in the face as she struggled to pull herself free.

Shiye was sizing up the situation. He took a careful step sideways, watching Matchitehew out of the corner of his eye. Hassun had eyes for no one but Shiye.

"Tiponi never loved anyone other than herself," Shiye growled. He could see a thin trail of blood trickling from the place where Hassun held his knife to Dianna's pale skin. He was trying not to panic.

"Enough of your lies," Hassun snarled. "You besmirch her name with the air from your lungs. You do not deserve to utter it."

Matchitehew was sliding away from them. Hassun's crazed eyes darted to him and he pointed his blade at him, his hair sticking up all over his head. "You move, and she dies," he said. He pulled hard on Dianna's arm. She winced, but no sound of pain escaped her lips. She looked furious. Defiant.

It was one of the many things he loved about his wife. She would not cower from a threat. She would tell Shiye later how terrified she had been. Later, when they were alone. She would not show weakness in the face of an enemy.

Shiye held up his hands in a gesture that showed his willingness to comply. "Let's talk about this."

"You're through talking," spat Hassun. He tightened his grip on Dianna's arm, his blade digging viciously into her neck. She choked, and he laughed. It was an insane laughter. He looked mad. Quite as mad as his wife had looked moments before she had fallen to her death. And suddenly, Shiye knew what was going to happen before it did.

Matchitehew lunged at Hassun, jabbing his knife into Hassun's side and causing him to yell with shock and outrage. Dianna threw her elbow into the wound and Hassun yelled even louder. He stumbled, released Dianna, and then he lunged at her with an animalistic growl of ferocity.

Shiye ran forward, ducked, and barreled his shoulder into the man's midriff.

Hassun stumbled back again and nearly fell. Then he turned, took hold of Rose's tiny shoulders and heaved her, shrieking, off of the back of the horse.

A blade, thrown by Dianna with deadly accuracy, flew by Shiye's ear. Hassun's yell of fury echoed back to them through the surrounding trees. Shiye ran forward as Hassun's grip weakened, tugging Rose from his grasping fingers.

Hassun lunged again, but Matchitehew had thrown himself recklessly onto the man's back in his efforts to protect Rose.

Shiye tripped away from the struggling pair, his daughter safe in his arms once more. Hassun turned on Matchitehew. "You are a traitor!" he screamed, clawing at his face with gnarled fingernails. "You—" but Matchitehew had shoved himself away from Hassun, whose eyes went wide as he lost his balance on a large, icy stone underfoot. His arms pinwheeled madly, and then he fell.

There was a sickening crunch, and Little Rose hid her face in Shiye's chest.

Hassun had fallen backward onto Shiye's dropped blade. He was dead.

Chapter Sixteen

A stunned silence rang around them, filling all the empty space with its unwanted presence. Little Rose was sobbing into his shirt. Her grip was nearly strangling him.

"Shh, Rose," Shiye whispered shakily, patting his daughter's back with a hand that felt numb. The touch of Dianna's fingers on his forearm made him jump.

"You're bleeding," she said.

As she led him off to the side of the path, the pain seemed to hit Shiye in full-force. He gasped as his shoulder began to throb and he had to set Rose carefully on her feet. Her dress was stained with the blood from his injury. She was trembling, and Shiye did not remove his good arm from around her shoulders as Dianna set about tending the wound.

Sounds of scuffling met his ears. Out of the corner of his eye, he saw Matchitehew dragging Hassun's body away into the trees. He winced as Dianna's gentle fingers probed the gaping hole left by the arrow in his shoulder.

"It's deep," she said, her voice conveying her disquiet. "We may have to cauterize it to get it to stop bleeding."

Shiye frowned in distaste, but, glancing down at his pale fingers, knew Dianna was probably right. The snow around them was spattered with droplets of his blood. It stood out starkly against the backdrop of white.

Rose had stopped crying, but she was still shivering. Huddling close to his side as Dianna sat about starting a fire, she looked like a lost puppy. Her eyes were wide and sad.

Shiye bent down and kissed the top of his daughter's head. "I'm sorry I went away," she whispered, turning her sweet face to look up at him. "I wish we had stayed with Grandpa, and Grandma, and my aunties, and uncles, and cousins."

Sunlight lanced across her caramel-colored skin, leaving a pale glimmer in its wake. The dappled light of the trees created splotches of light over them all.

"We will see them again, Rose," Dianna said. "They may be heading the same way we are."

Matchitehew approached them slowly. His hands and clothes were covered in a thin layer of mud.

"I took him a little ways off the path," he muttered so only Shiye could hear him. "I buried him. Here's your knife."

Shiye eyed the blade as Matchitehew handed it back to him, watching it catch the light. How had that happened? he wondered, replaying the scene over and over again in his mind. How had his blade come to be standing just so...? It was impossible.

He sighed and tucked the knife back into its sheath. This was not the time to ponder the peculiarities of fate and chance. He said a silent prayer of thanks, pressing another kiss to the top of Rose's head.

Dianna was heating the blade of a throwing knife on the small fire she had somehow kindled to life. She looked up at him. "Ready?" she asked. Shiye grimaced, pulled his arm from around his daughter's shoulders, and urged her stand.

"Take her into the trees for a bit," he said to Matchitehew. "Don't let her see." Rose had been through enough that day without having to witness her mother scorching his wound closed with a hot knife. Matchitehew looked taken aback.

In truth, his decision to allow Rose out of his sight with Matchitehew surprised even himself. But he had seen the look on Matchitehew's face as he had thrown his body on Hassun to protect Rose. Something had shifted in their dynamic. He had earned, if not Shiye's forgiveness, then at least his trust. He could tell by the way Dianna was looking at him, that she felt the same way. Matchitehew had proven to them that he meant what he had said. He would protect them. Shiye was absurdly comforted by the thought.

He didn't have much time to dwell on the matter, however. Dianna was facing him, looking business-like. Her face was blazing and fierce.

"I love you," she said, leaning forward to press her lips to his. He supposed she meant it to be a brief, fortifying touch of their lips, but before he knew what had happened, their kiss had deepened into something neither of them could control.

Shiye lost himself in the sensation of her lips on his. It was a moment suspended in time. Everything around him had stopped, and there was nothing but Dianna. The feel of her as she leaned into him, cautious of his injury, but insistent. For that moment, he was able to forget. He forgot the sting of the hot blade that was coming, the things they had been through, and how very far they still had to go. He forgot that he was in horrible pain. That his fingers were tingling with numbness and his body was trembling with exhaustion. He forgot it all and held his wife to him in a kiss that defied every horrible experience they had been through. He found joy in her touch.

When she pulled away from him, he tugged her back. His mouth devoured hers with fervor. Quite suddenly, his wife began to sob.

Shiye let her tears run down his cheeks for a moment before pulling back and tucking her beneath his chin. The fierce protectiveness he'd always felt towards Dianna was surging through his veins like fire.

"We're alright," he whispered to her, rocking back and forward slightly. "We're all alright."

"I know we are," she said, at last, recovering herself enough to look him directly in the eye.

He held her gaze, using his good hand to brush cold fingers over her damp cheeks. Dianna leaned her face into his palm. "I am so proud to be yours," she told him.

"You will forever be mine," he responded. Shiye straightened as his eyes fell onto the knife that still lay in the embers of the low fire. He sighed, then sat back resignedly, pulling open his shirt sleeve. "Let's get this over with."

They arrived in Hunton's Ranch to an unusual blaze of warm winter sunshine. Their shadows drew out in front of them like a phantom parade as they made their way through the busy town in a haze of tiredness.

"Where are we going, Mama?"

Dianna looked over at Little Rose, who was watching the many buildings they passed with glazed eyes. Her head was bobbing gently against Shiye's chest, swaying with the movement of the horse.

"To the train station and then the post office," Dianna answered. She scrubbed her hand over her eyes, trying to ignore the way her thighs chafed uncomfortably against the saddle.

"Why?"

"We're going to leave a message for your aunties."

"They did say they were coming, didn't they? I would think they would already be here by now," grumbled Shiye. He looked around conspicuously, as though expecting his in-laws to materialize from behind a bookshop.

"I don't know," sighed Dianna. "They said they'd be right behind us, but we left in such a hurry..." she glanced at her daughter, remembering the weeks of panic she'd endured as they followed Matchitehew half-way across the country in pursuit of her. "I told them where to go," she said finally.

Matchitehew followed them quietly, his expression mild and indifferent.

They reached the train station at a quarter past ten and the others waited while Dianna approached the counter. "I'm looking for my family. They would have arrived off the train sometime within the last week. They might have asked for me?"

The man behind the counter grunted. "I wouldn't be quick to forget them," he said irritably. "Bossy sort of woman? Came with a load of other people? All clamoring about a blonde and an Indian man?" His eyes flickered to Shiye, who stood a few feet away.

Dianna smiled "That would be them, sir."

He frowned unconcernedly, scratching at his receding hairline. "They arrived here on Thursday. When I told them I hadn't seen ya, they headed to O'Lawry's to rent a coach and some horses."

Dianna's brow furrowed. "Did they leave a message for me?"

The man behind the counter looked as though he was quite ready to be rid of her. He stood up, grumbling audibly, and made his way to a file on the desk behind him, hitching up his trousers as he went.

"Let's see. Thursday. Thursday," he mumbled, flipping resignedly through a stack of paper. He lifted a small piece of parchment out from the rest and looked at it intently. "This for you?" he asked, holding it out at last.

Dianna took the note.

Dianna,
We will head towards Buffalo Creek. If we cannot find your homestead, we will meet you in town. I hope all is well.
-Mother

Dianna sighed and crumpled up the paper. Her mother was not one to dawdle. The family would likely be waiting for them in Buffalo Creek. *I hope all is well.* Dianna wondered how much it had cost her mother to write that simple sentence.

She thanked the station attendant and walked back over to her family.

"They arrived on Thursday," she said. Try as she might, she couldn't remember what day she and Shiye had arrived in Hunton's Ranch. The journey back from Manhattan was a mindless blur of dread and haste. "They're waiting for us."

Shiye rolled his eyes. "So we should have gone home," he said grumpily. Dianna cast him a stern look and he winked at her. "On we go then?"

It was several days more before they began drawing close to their home. The winter continued to be mild and there was a hint of Spring in the cool air. The sunlight was warm on their backs as they passed by familiar landmarks. Dianna could feel a small, hopeful bubble burgeoning to life within her. They were going home. Home to the place she had built with Shiye. The place she had thought that she would never see again.

"Is that smoke?" Dianna said suddenly. They had just rounded a bend. All that stood between them and their little cabin was a pasture dotted with snow and a downhill slope. Dianna was suddenly reminded of the dream she had had so many long months ago. A dream of fire. She shivered as she pointed. "There. Do you see it?"

The rest of the party halted, their eyes scanning the skyline. "It's coming from the house," Shiye said, sounding startled. Without another word, all three of them kicked their horses forward. They galloped across the field, cantering to a halt next to the barn. Shiye dismounted first, looking around.

The smoke, Dianna saw, was unfurling in slow spirals from the chimney. Shiye raised his hand to signal them to wait and Dianna watched him approach with apprehension on her face. Had someone taken up residence while they were away?

The front door opened before Shiye could reach it however, and a thin trickle of smoke leaked out of the corners. A woman emerged, coughing, her hands over her face, shortly followed by three others. All of them with their hands covering their mouths.

"Good gracious, Mother," said a familiar female voice, "What on Earth did you put in that pot?"

Samantha Brittler pulled her hands away from her face, looking extremely annoyed. She opened her mouth to respond to Noelle, but then caught sight of Shiye, standing feet away from the others.

"Oh, there you are!" she exclaimed, gathering her heavy, black skirts about her ankles and coming over to meet Dianna as she slipped from her horse's back.

"Mother!" Dianna cried, striding forward to greet her. But to everyone's surprise, Samantha Brittler moved past her daughter. Her eyes, Dianna saw as she turned around, were entirely focused on Little Rose. Dianna's mouth opened with astonishment as she watched her mother pull Rose gently from the saddle and wrap her arms around her.

Rose was looking unnerved by her grandmother's sudden display of affection. She wrinkled her nose in confusion and held her little arms rigid at her sides with shock.

"My dear," said Samantha, pulling away from Rose to brush a dark strand of hair away from her eyes. "Thank heavens you're alright."

Rose's lips tweaked up in the corner as she examined her grandmother with a critical gaze. Then, evidently having come to a decision, she bent forward and wrapped her arms around her.

Dianna felt tears spring into her eyes as she heard her daughter whisper:

"I'm glad you like me now, grandmother."

Samantha Brittler huffed indignantly as she stood up, straightening her frumpled skirts, and gave Rose a small pat on the head. Rose smiled up at her sweetly, then she turned to greet her Aunt Noelle, who had moved forward and waited patiently beside the pair.

"Where did you go, little one?" Noelle squeaked, holding back tears. "You had us all so terribly worried."

"I went on an adventure with my friend, Chew," said Rose happily, gesturing to Matchitehew, who was now standing a good distance away, looking awkward.

This statement made Samantha raise her eyebrows at her eldest daughter, but Dianna said: "I'll explain later."

Samantha did not appear to think much of this, but she was distracted almost instantly as Thomas Brittler stepped out of the cabin.

"Well, I think I put out the worst of it," he said, looking highly disconcerted. "I hope Dianna has...Di?" he had just noticed the newcomers. Dianna flew to him at once and wrapped her arms around her father.

"Oh, Father. You shouldn't have come!" she proclaimed, taking a step back from him. Thomas Brittler looked offended at the very idea.

"Not come?" he asked irritably. "How could I not have come when my granddaughter was in danger?" He looked around at the surrounding people and his eyes found Rose. "Here she is!" he shouted jovially. "My darling girl. We were so worried." Rose ran to him and he embraced her with such enthusiasm that he lifted her off the ground. "Shame on you," Thomas said, holding his granddaughter close. "Shame on you for worrying us so."

Dianna's eyes found the fourth addition to their group. Kenneth Black had remained silent throughout the reunion, but now he cleared his throat and looked pointedly at Shiye and Dianna.

"What happened?" he asked. His knowing eyes darted to Matchitehew and back again. "What's been going on? We didn't know what to do for the best. Whether to wait here for you or start up a search."

Dianna sighed and looked around at Matchitehew, who bowed his head.

"I'll put up the horses," he said. He took hold of Tawny and Tanulonli's reins and lead them toward the barn, his shoulders heavy with the weight of his guilt.

LITTLE ROSE | 161

It took several hours to explain what had happened. When they had finally succeeded in answering most her family's many questions, Dianna had a few of her own.

"But where is Sarah? What happened after we left? What did you all do?"

"I was hard put to stop your father from riding out after you," said Samantha Brittler. She was standing in Dianna's tiny kitchen, her hands busy as she chopped many of the vegetables she had found in the food cellar.

Dianna registered how odd it was to see her mother standing in her home, let alone in her kitchen. Her dark hair was pinned loosely onto the top of her head, and she looked more relaxed than Dianna had ever seen her. It was odd. As though her two lives had come together in some strange, irreversible way.

"I wanted to come after you," growled Thomas. He looked over at Shiye. "I would have ridden with you to find her."

"I know you would have," said Shiye with a raw smile, "That is why I took special care not to inform you that we were leaving."

Thomas Brittler frowned at his son-in-law, but the rest laughed.

Kenneth said: "I wish I would have been there when it happened."

But Shiye shook his head. "There was no way of telling that Matchitehew would follow us so far. None of us could have done anything to prevent this." He reached for his daughter's small hand. "What matters most is that she is safe. We are all safe now."

"But where are Sarah and Charlotte?" insisted Dianna. "Why did they stay behind?"

"Charlotte, Sarah, and her husband are supervising the gathering all of our things," said

Samantha sharply. The tone of her voice suggested she disapproved of what she was about to say next. "We are moving to Wyoming."

A shocked silence followed this pronouncement. Dianna stared from her mother to her father, to Noelle, who was grinning broadly. "Your Father has deemed it an acceptable place to begin cultivating his third outpost of Brittler Steal. He has already purchased a portion of suitable land from the government. We begin building in the Spring."

Dianna's mouth fell open. Thomas Brittler began to chuckle.

"But-but your house," Dianna choked, still looking from one face to the next. "Your lives. Manhattan..."

"A small price to pay to have all of our family in one place," whispered Samantha Brittler. Dianna looked at her. And she thought she could see a glint of amusement in her mother's perpetually unamused expression.

Dianna got up from the table and hugged her. She tried to inject many unspoken things into the embrace, and perhaps her mother understood.

Kenneth and Shiye began talking excitedly as Dianna released her mother, whose smile had never looked so genuine.

"If Wyoming is where this part of your heart lies," Samantha whispered, cupping Dianna's face in her hand, "then the rest of your heart will follow."

Dianna burst into tears. Shiye looked up at her from where he sat at the table and smiled.

"I quite like the idea of a working ranch," Kenneth was saying to Thomas and Shiye. "Once the house is built, perhaps we can look into purchasing some cattle..."

Epilogue

The big house on the hill stood out starkly in the early-morning brightness, its white walls and shutters glimmered enchantingly in the golden light of the sunrise. The inhabitants of Buffalo Creek often admired it from afar, many with pride in their voice, having helped the well-to-do owner of the steel mill build the place for his well-to-do family.

They were an odd bunch, these high-ranking members of Manhattan society. For one thing, the eldest daughter was married to an Indian man. Many people had seen them together in town, arm-in-arm, chatting animatedly with their young daughter, Rose. It was very peculiar to see a redskin man in clothing of such fine quality.

The townspeople often shook their heads at such a relationship, but none of them could ever have a bad thing to say about the unusual couple, as they were both unfailingly kind. Their daughter, Rose, was amongst the more polite and respectful children of the town, keen to bring a smile to the face of a stranger.

The owner of the steel mill, Thomas Brittler, was an odd man as well. He was often to be seen sporting an impeccably tailored suit and riding over the top the hills at six in the morning. Which was what he was doing now, of course.

Dianna sat back in her chair on the front porch and watched as her father's horse cantered to a stop on the top of the nearest hill. She raised her hand and gave him a sarcastic salute, then cupped her fingers around her lips. "Your breakfast will be cold again," she shouted at him. He grinned and tugged his prized stallion in a circle.

"Save me something, won't you?" he yelled back to her.

Dianna shook her head, her lips pursed in amusement.

She did not hear her husband come up behind her, but she could feel his warmth before he spoke.

"Now that's a beautiful sight," he said. Dianna looked out at the sunrise as it spilled over the tops of the nearby mountains.

"Yes it is," she whispered. She glanced up at Shiye, expecting him to be admiring the same view, but his eyes were fixed on her face.

"Look at you," he murmured, tracing a rough finger over the smooth skin of her cheek. "You're so beautiful."

Dianna blushed and stood, brushing her blonde hair away from her eyes. "I am lucky that I married a man with such terrible eyesight," she joked. "Perhaps he will never see me age."

"You will always be beautiful," he said, and he bent to press his lips tenderly against her own. Dianna sighed and let Shiye's comforting, warm embrace envelope her like the heat of a blazing fire.

Together, they turned to watch the sun as it flooded the morning sky with brilliant color.

Once, a long time ago, Dianna had ached for adventure... and she'd found him. He made her heart pound with the touch of his hand and gave her spirit wings so that she could soar alongside him and be his.

Dianna turned her face to the glow of the sun and closed her eyes. She felt the heat of it radiate into her skin. What a glorious day it was going to be.

The End

Do you like Historical Romance?

The Rumor Mill is a group of likeminded individuals that all share a passion for the historical romance genre. Join *Josephine Blake* and over 900 other authors and readers in creating a friendly, creative, and fun atmosphere where you can participate in giveaways, win free prizes and help the authors brainstorm about their newest writing projects. Be part of the story.

Join Us on Facebook!

The Rumor Mill
Finest Historical Romance

JOSEPHINE BLAKE is a historical romance author who enjoys a quiet life on the outskirts of Portland, OR. Her debut novel, Dianna, hit the shelves in August of 2016.

Before publishing her own work, she worked as a freelance fiction and ghostwriter for numerous clients. Josephine Blake is happily married and freely admits that her husband is the inspiration for every bit of romance she ever writes.

She lives with her delightfully charming husband and a Persian kitty named Ruby. Both are equally feisty. When she's not writing, she's chasing her nieces and nephews, spending time with her family, or thinking about what to write next!
She'd love to hear from you. Shoot her an email at:

admin@awordfromjosephineblake.com

or

Sign up for her newsletter by visiting her website to receive a free download of:

The Heart of Hope
A Companion Short Story for Dianna

You will also receive occasional updates on sales, new releases and freebies!

www.awordfromjosephineblake.com

Made in the USA
Columbia, SC
11 May 2017